Utmost Love

Dark & Light-shade Emotions

Tanya Frew

Copyright © 2016 by Tanya Frew.

Library of Congress Control Number:		2015914115
ISBN:	Hardcover	978-1-5144-6305-5
	Softcover	978-1-5144-6304-8
	eBook	978-1-5144-6303-1

All rights reserved. No part of this book may be reproduced or transmitted in any form or by any means, electronic or mechanical, including photocopying, recording, or by any information storage and retrieval system, without permission in writing from the copyright owner.

This is a work of fiction. Names, characters, places and incidents either are the product of the author's imagination or are used fictitiously, and any resemblance to any actual persons, living or dead, events, or locales is entirely coincidental.

Any people depicted in stock imagery provided by Thinkstock are models, and such images are being used for illustrative purposes only. Certain stock imagery © Thinkstock.

Print information available on the last page.

Rev. date: 05/23/2016

To order additional copies of this book, contact:
Xlibris
800-056-3182
www.Xlibrispublishing.co.uk
Orders@Xlibrispublishing.co.uk

722616

Contents

Dedication v

Preface vii

Introduction xvii

Chapter 1   Dark shade emotions 1

Chapter 2   A dark eye in the white clouds 10

Chapter 3   Life changes, everything changes 20

Chapter 4   The pain no one else sees 30

Chapter 5   Decision making 36

Chapter 6   Looking to the future – a prince for Jan 50

Chapter 7   A good life: Light shade emotions 62

Chapter 8   Brink of emotional destruction: Motor Neuron Disease ... 72

Chapter 9   A dying wish 80

Chapter 10   Utmost Love 88

Chapter 11   Poetry speaks volume 101

Chapter 12   A Letter to my husband and our three sons 104

You are the oxygen, I breathe,
Cool and fresh, like the early morning breeze.
You are my best friends, my central heartbeat,
You are my constant lights, my stars,
My joy and my peace.
No matter where you are,
Just the thought of you,
Puts the brightest smiles on my face,
The one thing, I wear best – going place to place.
You uplift me, in every possible way,
I'm so glad you are here – to brighten my days.
Boys, you are my world, and the best of what life gives.
Joshua, Jaden & Javier

Auntie Clover, a special aunt you are – selfless and wise,
Most loyal and lovable, I treasure you so much,
Because of your inner-beauty,
And your incredible, sense of touch.
Over the years, you are there for me,
Sometimes I wonder, how different my life would have been,
If you haven't loved, and cared unconditionally.
You watched me grow up, into the woman I am today,
And believed in me, every step of the way.
No matter the challenges, I may be up against,
Or just when I'm captivated, by self-doubts,
Your love, strengthened me.
And these are only a few reasons, why I love you so much.

Dedication

This book is written, in honour of my absent mum – Hazel Green-Bent.

Dedicated to my love ones, who entirely captured my heart and my world. Husband Robin, our three most wonderful, precious and beautiful sons, Joshua, Jaden and Javier. My aunt Clover Green-Baltrip and dad Derrick Bent. I love you all, beyond your natural imagination.

Special thanks to

My supportive family, God mother Judith Lake-Johnson, Esther Rhone, Camiel Morgan, Andrea McKay-Phillips, Terry & June Hartery, Elin Barnett, Rainford Brown, David Nsaidoo-Storph, Cynthia Williams, Carol Sneddon, Marie Slattery and Maria McCarthy.

Endless love to my siblings, nieces and nephews.

Love gives the best of everything,
No matter how simple, it may seem,
Happiness, it surely aims to bring.
Whether you are heavy laden, with your burdens,
Or light as feathers, on the birds that sing,
Love is the best thing.
Have you a reason to toil, for far too many hours?
Or walk exhaustingly, for uncountable miles,
Till, sweat runs from the crown of your head,
Through your brows – and down to your toes?
Still, you do it all with plenty of smiles,
Knowing love is the reason, for such a thing.
Love powers the wind, beneath our wings,
So, we can rise up – and overcome,
The trials and crosses, we've succumbed.
Love is what the heart feels,
When true desires are fulfilled.

Preface

Love is only the simplest language, to understand. Yet, so many people struggle to comprehend. Quite often, some people don't even know what love is. Never experienced it – and so, never shared it. Others may have experienced love, either partially or in its full glory. At times, they want it to mean something – and other times, they want it to mean nothing. It all depends on their own unique experience, with this little and so effective word. With no experience of what love really is, it can be quite often misunderstood, and its power underestimated.

After completing my degrees in psychology, I have spent my entire lifetime, trying to understand the way in which we conceptualise love. Of course, I'm talking about pragma love (couples who share love, in a mature and realistic manner. For instance, long-term partnership or marriage). I have spent years and even now, talking to people, reading letters and offering advice (some, I have shared). Most times, I am thrown by some people's perception and experience of love. Especially, when their circumstances are unconventional, or simply downright intolerable.

Real life experiences

Two days ago, whilst I was at the park admiring the different ways, in which couples expressed love to each other. I got talking with a random couple – we spoke about, what love really meant to them. They suggested, love means friendship, and friendship means love. From the lady's perspective, love is when she stayed loyal to her husband, whom she hadn't been intimate with for several years. It was as a result of his erectile dysfunction – due to alcohol dependency, which restricted his blood flow. Ten years of marriage, and she could count the few and far in between, passionate moments they shared. Yet, they maintained a reciprocal and committed relationship.

Last night, I received a WhatsApp message, from one of my younger cousins. The longest text, he had ever written. Usually, he's not one for words, so I was quite surprised.

Hey T,

What's up? I really need someone to talk with… I've been feeling down for about a month now. I can't eat or sleep – a bit of a nightmare situation. Been in love many times, of which I've previously shared with you. But right now, it's different. I love my Angel, never have I loved any other girl like this. The love I give her, is simply the deepest, and I really don't want to lose her. Few weeks ago, she hurts me really bad – I've been holding it in, but it's just wrecking me. It's as if, my heart got minced, thrown to the ground, and then ran over by an overloaded double decker bus. Cuz, I feel the need to cry, cry, cry… It's unbelievable that I could feel such pain, purely on the basis of love – and it's not death. Well, maybe a part of me is killed off. I should contemplate a burial ceremony, this could be what's needed. Must I blame myself for loving someone this much? Please reply soon. Love, Denny.

Hi Denny,

I'm deeply sorry, for you what you are experiencing. From what you've said, can I guess what she has done…? Slept with another man? You know, I'm here for you, anytime. I will lend you my ears, and you just got to imagine my shoulders are next to yours – to support and embrace. You should cry though, if you feel like it. Hold your pillow as tight as you can, and squeeze it with all you've got, and let it out. I have been there too – wore the same tight shoes, and wondered if the pain would ever go away. And one day, it surely did! I was delighted, when it all past; and I was at my happiest again. But only with time.

My advice to you – don't do anything silly. Take time to process your feelings, before you make any decision. At some point in life, you will be hurt by your most-loved and dearest. But if there's a way, where both of you could sit down and talk, that would be great. Find out why, she did it. You will find, this might clear up any misunderstanding, on either or both parties. Perhaps, it doesn't seem likely now, but trust me, it would be the start of your healing processes. Then I suppose, you can take it from there. In the end, you may have to make a decision – whether you both kiss and make up, or say your goodbyes. However, if there's forgiveness, don't raise this issue with her again. It must stay in the past! This way, it's a fresh start. In every good relationship, love, trust, loyalty, honesty, openness and good communication are prominent. If you like, I would be happy to talk with her. But only if you give permission, to discuss such personal affair.

PS. Though your heart is very sore at the moment, you mustn't be too hard on yourself. Right now, you just need to focus on how to start feeling good again. I find that vigorous exercise, can be therapeutic. It gets the adrenaline running – and act as a natural mood-lifter. Perhaps, it might be the sort of remedying your mind needs, to give you a restful night. And set you up with sufficient energy, to go through the next day – possibly the rest of the week. X

Denny replied.

Hey T,

Sure, go right ahead and catch up with her. She trusts you, I know she won't mind... Although I'm not so sure, I can ever trust her again. I don't know... I really don't... The truth is, I don't even know if I will love any other, this much again. To trust her so much, with the most delicate part of me, and watched her smashed it – as if I'm made of stone, is pretty heartless and cruel. Surely, this can't be her way of showing true love. I might stay single after this – I'm just so hurt!!!

Angel and I correspondences

Hi Angel,

 Hope you are well. Sorry for the emotional struggles, you're facing at the moment. Denny asked me, to catch up with you. But I really don't want to do this, if you're feeling uncomfortable about it. Having said that, I'm not here to judge either of you, just to listen and understand, your emotional situation. X

Hi Tanya,

 Yes, we're struggling. We've been for some time now. I've done something terrible... Only once... And believe me, I'm paying for it. I'm feeling deeply hurt and ashamed, to see I was capable of hurting someone, I love. It was a very silly and selfish act – and I was caught up in my own world. I had confessed to him – because I didn't want to keep on lying. I know he loves me – I really do... But I also know, he will never trust me the same way again. Maybe if he gives us another chance, I will prove myself and promise – to not let this happen again. But everyone makes mistakes, right? No matter how big or small, we got to learn from them, and move on.

 The distance between us, made things crazy. But that's something we can work on, if we get that chance again. There are times, we know that we are doing something wrong, yet we persisted... Being fully aware, it isn't what you really want to do... Guilt is all I need to feel... Right? Tanya, thank you for talking to me today – I really needed it. Before your message, there was a thought that I might explode. I'm glad it didn't happen! Anyone could have experienced me at my worse. Another mistake avoided!! My anger is terrible, and can sometimes get the better of me. I didn't know, who to talk with about this sort of thing. My family and I, don't have the best relationship – and my friends? Well, put it this way, I wouldn't want them to judge me.

Oh, how different we expressed the same type of love? The same love that should protect us, from such emotional distraught, doth caused the deepest hurt. The type of pain, doctors can't cure. The type of pain that exist without a physical wound, still sensate so bad. Sometimes it seems emotional scars can be worse, and even more lasting, than physical wounds.

My lifelong friend Trish, shared her story.

Trish had a niggling thought, her ex-boyfriend Gav, was a serial cheat. Yet, she thought maybe... Just maybe, he wouldn't do it to her. Three weeks into their love bubble, Gav cheated with one of their best friends – just before he tried to get Daliah (Trish's other best friend) into bed. No success there! Trish forgave him after being reminded, she was the lady he introduced to everyone. Trish is the type, any decent man would like to have by his side. Yet, Gav needed to feel like the master to as many ladies, who could match their legs with his (not that I got the impression, he has a nice pair). But none of them was the trophy girl. Well, main-lady wasn't quite the trophy lady either. Sometimes, he wanted to lift Trish high as the heaven – and other times, he somewhat disgustingly spat at her. There was even, the occasional public humiliation. For instance, Gav had taken Trish to parties, alongside one of his other women. Once they arrived, Trish was totally ignored, like a bit filth by the wayside. As if that wasn't enough, Gav then took pleasure in sharing explicit sexual information, about his other women with Trish. She had cowardly listened, as her heart slowly curled in, like salt to a live slug. And in spite of this, she wasn't allowed to talk with anyone about it – or else...

Like any ordinary day, Trish went for a walk around her neighbourhood. She met a pregnant woman on her journey, and got talking. She thought this lady looked utterly ordinary. But before long, Trish heard a very heavy, wheezy breathing from her. She stopped and coughed. Trish stopped too, and offered a small bottle with water. The lady told her, she will be just fine, it was her asthma playing up. Trish commented on how neat her tummy looked – before curiously asked, how far along she was. The lady told her, nine months precisely. Their walk didn't get much further – her contraction had started. Trish encouraged her not to panic, and she was in safe hands. The lady was further away, from her own home. So, they went back to Trish's home, before calling the ambulance. Eventually, the ambulance came, although they didn't make it to the hospital, until after the birth. A baby boy was born on her living room floor. Alongside mother and baby, Trish got into the ambulance, and went to the hospital. She then excitingly asked the lady, about a name for her son.

"Travion Deli, after his dad's father," she joyously, responded.

"Travion Deli?" Trish, softly repeated.

Trish gently suggested, she rings her partner and share the good news. But the lady had left her mobile phone at home. Trish offered to make the call for her, if she knows the number – and so she did. The number was familiar to Trish, and most certainly Gav's name came up on screen. Trish, quite shockingly pressed the off button, and timely went back home.

After Gav got home, Trish asked about his new son – and he didn't deny. She told him it was over, her heart couldn't take any more... He suddenly held her down on the bedroom floor, sat on her stomach, and positioned a kitchen knife to cut her face. Gav told Trish, no one else could have her, except him. And, should she decide against their relationship, he would scar her beautiful face. Tears flooded her face, as she whispered "No, no, please... I'll stay with you." But eventually, she relocated to the city – without him knowing her whereabouts. Gav had rung hundreds of times, and asked her to come back. She went back, and there were no changes...

One evening, Trish went out with friends. But she was back home later, than Gav had expected. Therefore, this merited an enormous argument. Before she could say a word, he aggressively grabbed the collar of her top, pulled Trish towards him, and swiftly raised his hand in an attempt to slap her face. This time, she dug deep inside herself for a bit of courage – held him by his shirt collar, and positioned her arm to hit him. They were astonished by her action to fight back. Gav then gave Trish a very serious evil-gaze, before they walked away from each other. A moment later, she thought really long and hard, how to end their violent, abusive and loveless relationship – without anyone being physically hurt. Then she remembered, a friend had told her about a job in the city. Trish rang up about it – and was told to come in the next day, for a trial run. She went, and never returned... It was much happier days from there on – and most of all freedom... Freedom... What could be better? She finally chose happiness!

> If there's infidelity, then love is diminishing. Once love is in action – loyalty, faithfulness and trust are in place. If not, then there could be some love – but not in its fullness. Love in its full

glory gives satisfaction, fulfillment and reinforces commitment. Mum used to say, *love teaches patience and understanding*. And rightly so, it does indeed!

In this instant as I'm writing, a text message came in on my mobile phone. It was from one of my best friends. He was wishing me, happy Easter. Suddenly, I had a thought – I ought to ask him, what love means to him. And so, I did.

> *Wow! There are so many ways to define love... It's the love I give to myself, care, thoughts, kindness and respect. I share with my partner. She's the one I love best. I always give her my all. I share an infinite feeling with her, and it forever remains the same, no matter what. We share a great sense of joy, inner happiness and contentment. And I hope, she feels the same or even better. I never take her for granted, I just want to always keep her in a protective bubble.* He replied.

It was refreshing to hear, such an insightful expression of one's true feeling, for his utmost love. I don't think, it necessarily needs all the words in the English language to define it, even though it feels that way. There aren't too many words, as profound as love. In fact, it is the most intense, insightful and philosophical. Why does love seem so complicated, when it's also the simplest? Why is it so broadened, if it can be narrowed?

Several years ago, my neighbour Walter had consistently declared, his undying love for Cyndi. A lady he had met as a single mother, to her four-year-old twin daughters, Harris and Karris. Soon after they met, he asked her to move in with him. And so she did. They shared one double bedroom, also used as living and dining room. After a few months, Walter requested that Cyndi stop taking her contraceptives. Cyndi disagreed and told him, maybe a bit later. At that time, she didn't consider it a possibility, due to their financial situation. Walter started hitting Cyndi, and abused her really badly. A naïve Cyndi stood by him, as she clung to his famous words – I love you most.

Walter obsessively monitored all their finances, and Cyndi could only spend, whatever she was told to… One weekend, she went and visited her family in the country. Upon her return, she had noticed all her things were gone. Walter had sold, even the children's clothes, books and toys. All that was left, belonged to him. Walter explained that, he was securing their financial future. Though, how astonished Cyndi was, she was once again smoothed over with sweet words. Few days later, a Good Samaritan had given her some clothes, things and money. She was told to keep the money a secret, for emergency purposes. But she didn't. Walter then took the money away from Cyndi.

One day, her daughters were unwell, and the money was needed to pay for their health care. She asked him, if they could have a few thousand dollars. He told her no, because there was no money left. She didn't quite understood, at first. And so, she asked again. Walter told her, he had booked an all-inclusive holiday, in the Seychelles.

"Kiss my watsistnot (a term used instead of blatant swearing), please tell me you are joking," she said.

Cyndi felt very angry and upset – and decided to walk a 40 minute journey, to the hospital. But just then, there was a knocking at the door. It was a young girl about 16 years old, looked beautiful and was wearing an engagement ring. Walter took some deep breaths, before introducing his new fiancé. Cyndi shockingly opened her eyes and mouth wide, and repeatedly asked Walter why… He looked at her with no remorse, as he made her aware his fiancé was moving in. They took pity on Cyndi, and offered for her to stay the night. But most certainly, ought to be gone the next morning. She didn't accept their embarrassing offer, and so spent the night at the hospital. This was Cyndi's turning point – she went away and made a fresh start.

A few years later, Cyndi was happily engaged to a man, who was very ill, with a severe case of lungs and heart problems. Doctors had given up on him, but Cyndi didn't. He recovered after two years of trial treatments – and happily shared love, as love should be. Walter and his fiancé had four children together.

Where unconditional love reigns, infidelity is conquered.

Don't play with my emotions,
I really thought, you could see how much I love you,
But every time, you hold me close,

Thinking, you want to feel me near,
You pierced my heart, over and over again,
And filled it with despairs.
Don't play with my emotions,
As I've done nothing wrong, but fell in love you,
Ever since the day, I blessed my eyes on you.

Of all the things love is… It's certainly isn't hate, and neither is it a chore. Love is the most emphatic and common feeling shared – although everyone is affected by it differently. There is no doubt, love is amazingly incredible with profound depth, diversity and captivating power, with nothing to compare. Love embraces respect, care and consideration. It makes you want to lift that special someone, high in the clouds – in spite of, whether he or she can fulfill all your expectations. It makes you feel as if, your world is perfectly completed. Even when the flaws are high, as the Aconcagua Mountain, and deep as the Yarlung Zangbo Valley. If at last your love has come along, a genuine friendship will form. One that will put you at ease, to share even your deepest secrets. There will be no judgment, even if what is seen in you, is unexpected or surprisingly different…

What would we do without love? Our body is the temple of love. And if our temple is loveless, then most certainly, hurt, anger and pain will become its occupants. Amazingly, our heart is like an endless pit – there is always room for more. Love, wonderful love, makes us happy – and everyone loves to be happy!

People dealt with love issues in various ways. Sometimes, I get those who said to me, *"Oh, you can manage… I can't handle these situations… What can I do, if my love-life is failing, and I have kids to consider?"* I know, this sounds cut and dried. But I quite often say to people, your strength lies deep within you – and only you can reach it, no one else. If you don't pull it out – and amour your heart, surely the pain will last for a long time. Besides, you will be lying in an emotional pit of desperation, waiting to be helped by those, who rather dig your pit even deeper – then batter your heart until you are immune to the pain, they want you to feel. And of course, subjected to their deceits and obsession.

It's not selfish to be your best – even when others, don't appreciate your best. It's not selfish to want your partner, to make you feel the way, you make him or her feels. It's not selfish to choose utmost-love (happy and fulfilled love) over abuse. It's not selfish to choose happiness, for you and your kids – whatever that means to you. And it's definitely not selfish to choose YOU, if both of you can't stay together, enduring love in its full glory. Everyone, has an idea of what sadness and pain feel like. So happiness, is NOT that! Though how hard it might be to make some decisions, which will allow you to feel inner peace and contentment. It's that choice which will make the difference in your life, between enjoying utmost love and enduring loveless pain.

Be the first to love yourself, like no one cares,
Love you strongly, till there's nothing to compare…
Or else, others will wear you out,
And then leave you hanging, like an old dried-out trout.
Love yourself, from now till the end,
No matter how many times, life takes you around the bend.
Walk and talk with confidence,
Never mind those who snort at you,
While lazing on the fence.
Just be happy, loving you!
Tell yourself, you are attractive like the flowers in springtime,
You are beautiful inside and out,
And you will let your love speak volume,
Even when you are broken, and living without a dime.
Now, remember – love you, for who you are,
And then others, near or far,
Will love you, like an ever shining star.

Introduction

Utmost Love is a gripping love story, of Lady-Jan. Her journey from childhood into adulthood. She suffered the loss of her mother, at a very young age – and was brought up by her father, Jim. Ambitious and well-driven, she was a real credit to Jim. However, as Jan got older, she developed a fear of men, due to a traumatic childhood experience. Thus, she decided intimate relation wasn't to be – until she experienced her first inner feeling of falling in love. Eventually, Jan timely got over her fear, though struggled immensely to find true love. One day, her first love came along, but she discovered, he had an extremely rare genital dysfunction. In due course, reality had sunk in, and all were accepted. However, Jan's love life was like a roller coaster, which swirled around the eye of their tempest storm. Love aches and pain, were more paramount than the snow, on Snowdon Mountain in the heart of winter. Hence, the end of her first relationship.

Ultimately, she met and married her prince, Gui. Smooth like a serpent, he swept Jan off her feet. Though the devil himself, he was. A few years later, their lives were like a wrecked-ship, on the Atlantic Ocean's floor – because they were unable to have children. Trapped in a whirlwind of emotional events, their lives reflected the best and worst, of what true love really meant. At the pinnacle of their propinquity, divorce was imminent. Gui had a new family, although it was short lived – and he needed Jan more than ever. His partner and young child's mother, was diagnosed with motor neurone disease. Furthermore, an explosive secret was uncovered, and the police served justice. Was it the right decision, considering a young child's life was affected?

Finally, Jan had found her utmost love, John – and had a surprise biological family. Did Jan have her happy ending?

This book aims to give hope, in the darkest times. It will enlighten, and take you on a journey, where you will experience the thrills of ultimate love. It revealed different ways to love profoundly, in spite of pitfalls. This is what I called, *dark-shade emotions* – fear, loss, despair, guilt and loneliness. However, it is almost impossible to experience the fullness of love, without the lighter side – what I called *light-shade emotions*. It's fun, delightful, fascinating, interesting, toe-tipping-intense, climatic, joyous, sensational and certainly overwhelming! It gives contentment, inner peace, hope, and not forgetting the unfathomable sense of longing.

The story is partially based on real life experiences. Also, I drew on personal experience with individuals, unfortunately affected by Motor Neurone Disease. This is a condition that can affect anyone, at any stage of his or her life. Scientists are still trying to find out the real causes, and how to cure it. For now, it remains an incurable and untreatable condition. A lot of care and support are given, to allow these people to cope with MND. The final chapter, highlighted my utmost love.

I hope, some questions asked, is answered in this story.

CHAPTER 1

Dark shade emotions

Jan marvelled of the day, her prince will lay beside her in bed – to touch, honour and cherish her entire being. Blessed with all the attractiveness, some could only dream of – she confidently lived in her beauty. Tall and slender, with the most amazing bold green eyes. Long, straight, jet-black hair fallen below her shoulders – glowed even in the darkest night. Jan was very sophisticated, and was always well-dressed. She was never short of five and six inch heel footwear. Jan almost looked a bit too tall, and was hardly missed in a crowded place. On the note of stylish and beautiful, her home reflected just that too. A mansion fit for a queen, was located in one of the most opulent parts of Britain's countryside, South Leaside Way. A total of fourteen rooms, included a library, games room and a cinema. Her garden was the size of Manchester football pitch, and was completely private. It was filled with beautiful flowers, of all types – in a multitude of colours, meticulously arranged. It also boasted a steaming water fountain, which created the most serene atmosphere. The garden highlighted the splendours of nature, and was simply a cut above the rest.

Neighboured some celebrity homes, Jan enjoyed the grandeur of a well-kept community – with the advantage of splendid mountains, strikingly beautiful garden parks, and extraordinary calming lakes. This little earthly heaven, was just the place for Jan to get away, from the busy and combustible city – especially, after a long day at work. Jan wanted to enjoy a great life – however, peacefulness was key.

Jan embraced a hard working lifestyle, and had shown utmost commitment to her multi-million-pound fashion business. At about 8am, she could be seen most mornings, driving her big white jeep to work – and returned home, quite late some evenings. However, it wasn't hard-work and no play. Between 12-2pm, Jan had frequently joined her corporate friends, at the Whipmoore Restaurant and lounge – where she enjoyed games and laughter over lunch (crab tamale, roasted lamb and avocado salad, were her favourite). Dining out and having a big meal, was vital to Jan – as at home, there was no one to cook and share with. Nevertheless, most weeks wouldn't be completed, if Jan and 26-year-old Sandy (best friend, as well as neighbour), didn't fill their weekends, with all the luxury of a good life.

One weekend, Jan and Sandy went to Central London, on a short break. And of course, this meant some well-deserved ladies time and shopping. They talked about Victoria Secret, one of their much-loved stores. Sandy was interested in getting some fragrances, and possibly a few sports bras. Jan thought, she could buy some new nighties. After about half an hour in the supersize store, they had finally decided on taking their baskets up to the cash register. Sandy dipped into her bag to get her purse, but Jan was happy to pay for all.

"My treat," said Jan.

However, they couldn't help but noticed the handsome cocoa complexion gentleman, at the cash register. He looked at Jan and smiled flirtatiously.

"That will be £150 please," he spoke, pleasantly and professionally.

Jan paid, and smiled back at him, with a special twinkle in her eyes. Jan and Sandy made their way out – and just as they exited the store, Sandy pointed out the obvious... Jan, liked him.

"He is right up my street – so fit," Jan said, in a posh accent.

"Shouldn't you have left your number? Would you like me to go back, and give him one of your business cards?" Sandy said, in a funny, mischievous and inquisitive tone.

"Oh no! Then I would never be able to go back to VS, ever again," Jan replied.

"Uuum? Another opportunity missed, eeh Jan?" Said Sandy, endearingly.

They laughed and wandered around the shops a little longer, before decided to go for lunch.

"Where shall we go for lunch," Jan asked, with an unwavering look on her face.

"Depends on what we fancy. Something light for me," Sandy replied.
They tossed their thoughts for a while, until they finally decided…
"The Le Devoi place is good," Sandy said, persuasively.
"Great! Shall we go then?" Jan replied, decisively.

Only a few moments later, and they were pulled into the restaurant, by the delicate, indefinable and tantalizing smell, of freshly prepared food that fragrance the air. They ordered, and got stuck into cheese soufflés (served with double cream), water, juices, and an extra-large slice of pecan cake, to share. The ladies were having a great time as usual. However, Sandy couldn't help but noticed, there was a sudden change in Jan – she looked a little dimmed. Sandy curiously asked, if she was feeling OK. Jan spoke apologetically, before communicating some of her innermost thoughts. She had an overwhelming sense of loneliness, as she reflected on her past relationship. Jan really wanted to talk about it, and so Sandy gave her the chance to lighten her burden.

"Well, sit comfortably, fasten your seatbelt and get ready for take-off. Bear in mind, there might be some turbulence, but we'll eventually land safely. It's a slow ride, and a very long journey. Please feel free to snack away, while we revisit my past. After this, I bet you wished, you hadn't signed up to listen," Jan spoke, with a heavy sigh.

"Ready when you are, for take-off pilot Jan! I'll be your co-pilot for today – and you've got my full attention! Therefore, I'm happy to hold your hands and wipe your tears – if they come flowing down your cheeks, and blocked your views," Sandy spoke, in a funny pilot's sounding voice.

"Well, I will take the scenic route. Shall I?" Jan Responded.

They chuckled, before gracefully lifted their glasses, and drank some water. Jan then composed herself, took some deep breaths and shared her story.

Jan's story

As a little girl, Jan was always told not to talk to strangers, don't beg, and certainly do not accept drive from unfamiliar people. One day, they had moved homes, and Jim had left a few essentials at the old house. So Jan thought, she could go back and get them. Jim looked at her worryingly and couldn't help, but felt overprotective. Despite knowing, Jan was very smart and independent.

"I would get the things and straight back, dad."

"OK. But please safe. It shouldn't take more than about 30 minutes, there and back. Any longer than expected, I'll drive over and get you," Jim, spoke firmly.

Off she went, and stood at the bus stop. She waited a while, and didn't see a public transport coming her way. A while later, a black Toyota Camry approached… She stretched her arm forward – the car stopped. The front door swung open – Jan got in and shuts the door. She looked around nervously, but it was only them in the car.

"I should have let you sit in the back. But anyway, what's your name and where are you going?" The driver, asked.

"Ja-Jan," she said, quite timidly.

"Where did you say you were going?" He asked again.

"Only a few minutes up the road, sir – Hawk-way," she nervously replied, with a stiff smile. "Oh, alright… I won't go that far, but you could walk there, from where I'll leave you," he said.

"That's OK, sir. Thank you," said Jan. There was a pause between their conversations.

Then few minutes later, he gently caressed her hand. Jan shifted slightly, as there was a strong sense of fear and awkwardness. With no thought of holding back, he asked some very personal, uncomfortable and intrusive questions.

"So, you look about 15, are you a virgin…? Got a boyfriend…? Are you any good?"

Jan sat in silence – shocked and disgusted… But he wasn't giving up – and so once again, he repeated the questions, with the addition of another…

"Would you like to experience sex with me?" Jan, was utterly embarrassed.

"Boyfriend, sex…? I'm only 13 years old. You must be about 60?" She replied, in a horrified voice tone.

"Closed, 55. But you are not too young –" He said, quite calmly.

"I'm not a prostitute sir, and I couldn't tell you where to find one. I'm just a little girl, with big dreams, for me and my dad," Jan answered back.

He glanced at her, with a very focus, discourteous and weird look on his face.

"Oh dear, I've broken the most important rule. What have I done? What have I done?" Jan disquietly whispered to herself, as her body shivered.

"I'll will be diverting soon – stopping at my house."

"Oh no, how repulsive is this man?" Jan, quietly mumbled.

Jan's, stomach churned. She peed herself sitting down. She silently whispered a little prayer, and asked God for protection.

"Next right-turn, is the road to my house," he said, with a smug-ish look on his face.

"OK, sir. But I know my way, from where we are now. I would be alright to stop here, and walk it over to my old house – that's where I'm going. And my best friend, she's only living about five minutes away," Jan, responded in a trembling voice.

He did not look at her, or utter another word. Just as he was about to divert, he had accidentally driven the car into a wall. Frightened, though unhurt, she looked to see if he was OK, and he was.

"Stay in the car and don't move!" He said, quite sternly – with his dark moustache stuck out, as his knitted eyebrows flickered.

Jan knew, she couldn't afford to obey his injudicious advice. She swiftly took her seatbelt off, and attempted to open the car door – but was unable to do so. She then escaped through the window – before instantly, breathe a big sigh of relief. Jan watched him, stared at the car in despair – but she was just happy to be out safely.

Jan walked over to her best friend Kendri's home, and told her all... Kendri gave her a hug, and asked her mum to make them something to eat. Kendri's her mum made them ham sandwiches, and some freshly squeezed grapefruit juice. But soon after, it was time for Jan to go. She went straight to the old house, and found a small cloth bag with keepsakes. On her way back, she waited for the bus. But just as the bus approached, Jim drove up in his yellow Chevrolet. He queried why Jan was away, for such time. Jan somehow felt, it was best not to scare him, with all that had happened. Especially, she knew he would be very crossed. Jan only mentioned, she went by Kendri for a little while. Jim, looked at her and smiled. And every so often, glanced at her – with untainted fatherly love in his eyes, as they sang duets the whole journey back home.

Since that day, Jan had developed a fear of men. She was terrified, they would force her to have sex, before she was ready. But it still didn't stop her, from feeling some kind of attraction, to the opposite sex. Jan decided to wait, for as long as she could... At age 18, she started gaining confidence, and was timely getting over her fear. On Jan's 18th birthday, Jim asked her if she wasn't interested in boys. She told him yes – and that, she was more into boys now, more than ever. She was waiting for the right one, at the right time.

"It's a good thing, I don't have a boyfriend dad," Jan, said lightly.

"Why now?" Jim, curiously asked.

"Maybe, I would have been more distracted over the years. This could have impacted significantly, on my exam results. I had time to focus and achieved straight A's."

"Give your old man a cuddle. You're your mother's daughter alright. And, I… I'm just blessed to have you… Proud of you… You know that… Don't you?" Jim said.

"Anyway dad, I like someone," Jan voiced quite confidently, with glee.

"That's good! Tell me about him!" Jim, sounded excited.

"Don't worry, I won't disappoint you," Jan, assured Jim.

She looked at him and said, "Okay… Okay. It's Vaisy's Ethan."

"He's a good man," Jim said, with a very wide and happy smile on his face.

Jan and Ethan were the same age, with just months between their birthdays. Every morning they got on the number 45 bus, going to London city centre. It was never late, and they weren't either. Lower deck, left corner seat, right at the back, Ethan sat next to Jan. Their one hour journey to university, was somehow intense to start with. Neither of them would open their mouth, and say hello. The sideways glance and smile, did it for a while. Ladylike Jan, was happy to sit upright, crossed her legs and pretended to be reading her novel. Every now and again, she would look over her book, just for a glance. Ethan, could feel her eyes on him. Although he gave as good as he got.

One morning, Ethan got to the bus door, first in the queue. He went straight in, and seated himself, where Jan usually sat. She felt forced to sit in his seat. Unbelievable – she thought. Jan stared at the window – but there wasn't much of a view. Hundreds of people walked back and forth, trying to get to work, university or wherever… The windows, were mostly secured. Bottom window was sealed, without a handle. But above it, there was a smaller, rectangular-shaped window that, was opened – Ethan opened it even wider. Fresh air flowed through – he gently breathes in and out. They looked at each other, and gave an intense smile. Mint gums were at the ready, as Ethan broke the pack in halves and offered Jan.

"Thank you," Jan said politely, as she slowly glanced at him.

Ethan smiled, and offered her seat back.

"No, thanks. You're alright. Maybe, if I stay here," Jan, muttered subtly and sarcastically.

"Did you forget your usual seat this morning?" Jan asked.

"No, I really just wanted to break the ice with you," Ethan, voiced assertively.

Jan curiously inquired, if breaking the ice meant to say hello. Ethan quite promptly told her yes – before added that, they have been travelling on the same bus, to the same place for a while. It was time, they at least knew each other names. The conversation was in full flow all the way – mainly about fashion designing. Finally, the bus arrived at their destination – as they slowly walked through the main entrance, Ethan sang in a comical voice…

"Beautiful autumn day, lovely greenery… Would you care to join me for lunch today?"

She looked at him softly, before stroking her hair from front to back. Then came a pause. Ethan was about to say something, but Jan quickly replied, "Yes, OK. That sounds like a plan."

"At the greenery, then…?" Ethan, said. Then slowly swung himself around, and walked in the opposite direction.

Three hours later, it was lunch time. They met at the greenery as planned.

"A much better view here," said Ethan.

"Naturally beautiful and calm. Big flourished green trees, lovely evergreen-grass, beautiful pink, yellow, red and white flowers surrounded the gardens. I think there may be some white lilies too," Jan went on and on…

Ethan listened, in spite of that questioning look on his face. Okay – so you are fascinated by beautiful flowers, ah? They walked towards a wooden table and chairs – when suddenly, Jan caught up with herself, and explained apologetically.

"Oh, sorry – blown away by this side of the campus, I couldn't shut up! Usually, I go to the café or the hangout corner – next to the refectory."

"Yeah? This is my usual spot. Quiet and attractive, like…" Ethan, softly spoke.

He looked in her eyes, and held back from completing his sentence. An obvious non-smoking sign, nailed to a tree – was facing them. They noticed, and asked simultaneously, "Do you smoke?" Intrigued by their sameness in thoughts – they laughed flirtatiously, and nodded no.

"What's the point? When we can enjoy nice fresh air like this, without the smell of tar," Ethan uttered – as he stretched his hands forward (in a silly manner), and welcomed the lovely outdoors.

Sandwiches, were at the ready – Jan relished, her pickled ham and water; while Ethan savoured, his chicken mayo and ginger-ale. They spent their 60 minutes, engaged in good banter. But it was soon time, for their next lecture.

"Our lunch period is just about over. I have enjoyed lunch, and your company, of course," said Ethan, with a sound of cheerfulness.

"Ditto… We'll see each other at the bus stop. My art session might be longer this afternoon. Although, I could leave at the usual time. See you there then?" Jan replied.

It was an unusual day, though blissful. Ethan, was right up Jan's street. He had the smoothest of voice, just like runny honey on hot buns. Five feet six, slim built, and a smile to die for. Beautiful white teeth, lips of perfect proportion, and attractive grey-diamond eyes, cute and compelling – added to his physical attributes. Ethan, seemed to have only ever worn one hairstyle – head smooth as babies' bum cheeks. Ethan was a shy guy, though quietly confident in his profession. Even though, he wasn't exactly playing it too shy, when it comes to Jan. Nevertheless, Jan liked that, Ethan was a sight for sore eyes – alongside his gentlemanliness and sensitivity.

As time went by, their friendship grew – they were almost inseparable. A year to the day, since their friendship had begun. They were on their way to university, as usual – when approached the bus station, and noticed it was mobbed with people and polices, even soldiers. The roads ahead were blocked with traffic. People's faces were taut with despair. The sound of weeping and moaning was aloud in the air. People were heading in all directions, only to find a way out of the crowd. Jan and Ethan, gently pushed their way through, and discovered there was a major motor accident. A great number of people were seriously injured – and the buses were stalled. Getting to university for the day, seemed impossible.

Jan and Ethan, slowly made their way to a quieter spot, at a nearby play park. They sat on the swings, for a while, and shared an emotive moment. Teardrops fell from Jan's eyes – Ethan gently wiped her face, with his bare hand. They talked about the accident, and how interesting life can be – here today, gone tomorrow, sort of thing. This had brought their feelings into focus, as they decided to stop holding back, and go forward together.

Days followed were slow, as love flowed like the river Thames between them. Frequent visits were made to each other home – and their families were very pleased. Jan had a skip in her steps, and smiles to radiate the world. She glowed with happiness, like blooming flowers in the spring time.

Together, they had more dates, than Mr. Valentines had seen on February 14. Most evenings, they would find a place of solitude – anywhere, from the garden to the beach... All that mattered, were themselves in a world of love. In the winter times, outdoor spaces were still pretty special, there was no magic that their boots and coats couldn't do. Kept warmed with heaps of cuddles and kisses, relentless compliments and utter adoration, for each other.

They did an old fashion act, but it had worked for them – and was seemingly beautiful. Every parting moment, they had exchanged a written love quote. These were more treasure-able, than fancy gifts. Jan had kept hers into a little jewellery box – whilst Ethan had kept his, in a small wooden box. A few quotes were:

> *You showed me how to live and breathe love (Jan to Ethan).*
> *You are not just my dream, but my reality (Jan to Ethan).*
> *Love is all you are... You are all my love (Jan to Ethan).*
> *With you, I have everything I desired. Everything I ever needed (Jan to Ethan).*
> *With you, my heart will live on, even after I'm gone (Ethan to Jan).*
> *If losing myself in you, was all that love entails, then it's worth my life (Ethan to Jan).*
> *If every time I fall, I fell inside your heart – then I never want to stop falling (Ethan to Jan).*
> *My happiness lies in your heart, my peace in your eyes (Ethan to Jan).*

CHAPTER 2

A dark eye in the white clouds

Jan and Ethan were still sailing the love oceans. However, there was something significant, on Jan's mind. She wondered, if Ethan wasn't interested in a sexual relationship. Ethan didn't know, whether she was indeed a female. And at that stage, she presumed he would want to explore more. Unless, he had marriage in mind – in which case, Jan was happy to wait. But not for much longer, before she asked for advice. Late night radio six programs from 12-4, were all about love and relationships. Jan had phoned in, as an anonymous caller. She explained...

My boyfriend is the one for me – I am sure. But I often wondered, if he has the right amount of brain cells – or they are just under-active. It's been two years now, since we've been together – yet there was never a conversation about sex. He shows me immense love – and is always on time to assist my needs, except this very special one. But in quite an interesting way, it feels as if, he doesn't know how to have this conversation. However, he's quite a gentleman – and I love him. When the weather is at its best, we frequently go to Lakeside beach – to a secret spot. Once we arrived, he would flick-out a single flower for me. His shirt would be off his slender, smooth body, and used as our blanket, on the rough and gravelly shore. Our arms, a place of comfort – while we dreamt away. We listened to the sound of the ocean – as our eyes, now and again, glared at the sunlight far overhead.

Jan was advised, to communicate her feelings to Ethan, and give him time to be ready too. And so, she waited another five months. One very dark and cool mid summer's night, they were relaxing in Vaisy's old hammock – tied to the big, widespread Cercis Avondale Redbud tree. The sound of tranquillity filled the air, as they listened to each other heart beating rhythmically. Her body was getting closer and closer to Ethan's, he could hardly breathe. But he lay still, and wouldn't respond to her intimate signals. Suddenly, Jan took the bull by its horns, and started kissing him gently, then intensely. She lightly stroked his bared chest, consistently – until Ethan realised, Jan was ready, and she wasn't giving up. He raised his body, in upward position, and passionately kissed her – like never before.

"Oh, my darling, are you... Erm, sure?" He whispered in her ear.

"Yes, I'm sure. If not now, I don't know if I will ever be... So happy to proceed, when you are ready babe," Jan responded, impatiently.

"Maybe, if we could wait a bit longer. You're worth my wait – and I'll cherish you, for as long as life allows me to... I will always devote my love and loyalty to you, and only you, my lady," Ethan replied.

Jan was flattered, though felt a strange vibe... She held his face, and kissed him again. Ethan kissed her back – before telling her, there was something she needed to know. But he asked her kindly, not to run away or hate him – after she heard his story. Jan looked flushed for a moment. Then came a pause – a worrisome silence.

"Speak baby, please. My body aches, as I have waited for so long," Jan voiced, as she gently stroked his bottom lip.

He held her close once more and said, "I'm not like all men. I meant... I'm not all man. My body, I was born dif... Differently."

Jan looked mystified. She pulled herself away slightly.

"What do you mean?" She asked, astonishingly.

"Ma... My manly parts are all present. Just, I seem to have more than what's needed," he said, in a gentle and stuttered voice.

"Ethan, what are you trying to say? Please, say it out clearly!"

"I was born with male and female organs. I have never done this before either. So far, I've spent my whole life worrying about this day – when I opened up and told the love of my life, I don't know which to use. Despite this, I really do think I'm a man," Ethan explained.

"Oh My Gosh Ethan! Profound indeed. How very interesting?" Jan, spoke out furiously!

They sat upright in the hammock in silence, for a while. Neither of them knew precisely, what to say to each other. Eventually, Ethan asked Jan to say something.

"I don't know what to say – you could be a woman or a man? I need to think!! I need to think!!" Jan replied, sounded upset and confused.

"Why didn't you say, much sooner? I wouldn't judge – you know that! I love you too much, to be like that. I thought you trusted me enough, to share anything and everything. Have you thought of getting rid of the one, you might not want to use?"

"Yes, I've thought about many things, but I have done nothing. I am a man, a happy one with you. Not just when we are together, but it's also the way I always feel," Ethan spoke, persuasively.

"How would you know or decide on your sexuality, without some form of test?" Jan asked.

Ethan, felt very uneasy. He placed both hands, over his eyes and caressed them intensely. The silence hung between them, for about 20 minutes. Jan thought, maybe Ethan needed more time. She asked him to be honest, about what they should do from there on. Ethan suggested, it would be better to go to bed, and think about the night. It was later than usual for Jan to travel back home, so she stayed as planned. But it was relatively difficult, for both of them, whilst they lay apart in bed. Ethan entrusted Jan with the whole story, from birth. And although, Jan had never heard anything of such before, she listened keenly and took it all in.

Next day, Jan woke up at 5am. Briskly walked down the road, for about 15 minutes before slowing down. Just before the big deep corner, overlooking the abandoned valley, she stopped and stared away into a dream for a while. Naturally attractive green vegetation, cool breeze and a moment of peace, was certain. But that spot, wasn't one of her favourite places – it was a commonplace, for overturning vehicles. Thus, she made her way back. At the house, Ethan was awake, and met Jan at the door. They held hands, as Jan assured him things will be alright – the walk and fresh air had cleared her mind. Jan was now ready, to try and put things into perspective.

"Did you sleep, eventually?" They asked at the same time – as a little smile forced its way out...

Jan was ready to go home – Ethan walked with her. They thought some sleep would be beneficial – and so Ethan gently kissed her, good bye. Once Ethan arrived back home, he called Vaisy to the back conservatory – and told her, Jan knew... Vaisy empathised, and was happy Ethan at last, shared his secret. They justified their inner-feelings, with a tightly squeezed hug. So much so, they could feel each other heart beating. A very heavy sigh came out, as Vaisy wished his parents didn't run away and left him – just after he was born.

The weekend was over, and there was no contact from Jan, until Monday morning. It was the usual meeting point. Jan sat closer to Ethan, and shared his seat. She then softly whispered...

"It's alright with me, if you want to remain a man. Though if you chose to be a woman, I'm happy to be your best friend." A happy smile, slowly brightened their faces.

"I'm a man, just with more complications than other men. I will get rid of my female organs, the best I can. Will you be there with me?" Said Ethan, whilst gently clung to Jan's fingers.

"Of course, yes. You bet I will... All the way," she told him.

"Thank you, my dearest," Ethan whispered, as he kissed her hands.

At lunch, they had made plans to get closer. An old barn in the open lot, next door Ethan – was the perfect place for a romantic evening. Scented candles and fresh red rose petals, set the scene. Granny's homemade nibbles, water and a small basket of fresh fruits, were at the ready. And of course, the night wouldn't be perfect, without Jan's special snuggle-up blankets. Hence, their first night of pleasure. They slept in each other's arms, until about 6am. Their bodies couldn't get any closer to each, as they discussed the night's event. Who was nervous – stiffen – and just whom, weren't so shy after all. Once more, they embraced life, love and laughter.

The following weekend, Ethan and Jan walked six miles to the cinema. It was a delight, as they watched *Love is in the air part two*. Together they reminisced, as their eyes told a story of love and passion. After the movie, they walked a half of their journey – and the best part was a quick stop, at the candy-man shop. One extra-large cotton candy, shared between them. Ooh, how divine! Fingers and lips were covered with sweet, sticky candy floss, and the only thing between their beautiful smiles. Every moment was precious – and every opportunity to express love, was mutually embraced with gentle, physical gestures. On their way to the bus stop, they skipped, danced, and even stepped on each other toes. The wind blew softly, and the tree leaves rustled, as their minds strayed to love-wonderland. Once the bus arrived, it was a slow drive home. Gentleman-Ethan, ensured Lady-Jan was escorted to her door. Stood at the opened door, Ethan held Jan around her waist, ever so delicately. Then they sang a little duet, *Ta da da... Let my heart, stay with yours forever more*. The melody in their voices, were like that of nightingales – sensational! They sang with such conviction – any stone-heart, could have turned into melted butter.

"Goodnight my love, sleep well," Ethan whispered, and sealed with gentle kisses.

Ethan walked away, as Jan watched him hesitantly. About six feet out, she softly shouted, "Ethan!" He stopped. Jan went closer, held him tight, and kissed passionately. That was all he needed, to complete his night.

Life was as it should be for the young lovers. Jan and Ethan couldn't have been happier, although totally unprepared for the upcoming challenge. It was eight weeks on, since sex became a part of their relationship. Matured in their doings, sex usually happened on Jan's safe days. Therefore, contraception was never an option. Nevertheless, Jan had missed her menstrual cycle, and became very concerned. Jim wanted to be certain, so he bought her a pregnancy test straight away. Jan did it – the wait felt longer, than it should be. A nervous Jan, left the test on the toilet seat – while she prayed that it would be negative.

"uuuuum... uuuum... I have got another year left to complete my studies... Owh... Owh... Noo... I don't know about a baby now," Jan cried, whilst she shook her legs apprehensively.

Jim, knocked on the bathroom door. Jan let him in, and out she went without the result. Jim looked at it, and told her shockingly, "You are pregnant!" Her back against her bedroom door, she slid down to the floor.

"What to do now, dad? I am sorry... I have let you down. I wanted to make you so proud of me. I really didn't plan to have a baby so soon. I thought Ethan and I, were being super careful – but obviously not careful enough!" Jan, spoke and cried regretfully.

Jim confidently assured Jan, all will be well – and he will be right by her side, come what may. But first, she needed to talk with Ethan. Next day at university, she broke the news at lunchtime. Ethan's reaction was bittersweet. His career journey flashed in front of him. His face was flushed, by a wave of disappointment.

"A baby? How did we make a baby? I thought we were careful...?" He spoke softly.

"Maybe we haven't done a superb job, protecting ourselves," Jan voiced.

The donut shop, was only half a mile away. Surely, a couple of jammed donuts and hot drinks, were well deserved. As they revelled in their astonishment, Ethan asked to see the test result. Jan told him, she had left it at home, and didn't even looked at it herself. A mystified Ethan, felt curious. He questioned her again.

"Did you say, you haven't seen the test result?" He curiously, asked.

"Yes, I left it on the toilet seat at home. Dad told me the result was positive. But I had also missed my monthly... Once I had put the two together, I went straight into panic and distraught mode. I'm sorry Ethan," Jan, spoke tentatively.

Jan sat closer to Ethan, and quite placidly suggested, they go home and look at the test result together. He agreed. Ethan then assured her, whatever they had to do, they will do it together. On their way home, every man or woman with a baby became apparent. At times, they stopped and gazed at small babies lying in their buggies, as their minds wandered away. Back at Jan's home, Jim was delighted by the opportunity, to become a granddad. Even though, he had felt a strong sense of regret, for Jan and Ethan. Nonetheless, he overly imagined Jan and Ethan got married, and settled with their little family. But Jan had just about enough on her plate, and marriage wasn't on her mind. It didn't take Jim much time to put financial plans in place, for his new grandchild. He also hoped, when the baby comes, Jan and Ethan would allow him to help. So as to give them a chance, to complete their courses.

Jan and Ethan arrived home.

"Dad! Dad!" She softly, though eagerly shouted.

"Yes, in here...!" Jim shouted from the laundry room, at the back of the house.

"Where's the test result?" Jan, asked.

Jim told Jan, it was on top of the bathroom bin. Jan and Ethan had a look, and noticed there was only one line present. She wasn't pregnant after all. Ethan held her closely and kissed her cheeks. Jan turned to her dad and explain the test results – that it needed two lines to be positive. Maybe it was his wishful thought, in a good way, Jim told them – but he apologised for the false alarm. Jan felt she was to be blamed – and therefore, took responsibility for not checking the test result herself.

"Stay for dinner?" Jan, said to Ethan.

"No, I must be on my way home soon. Gran would be thinking of me," he replied.

"Alrighty, see you in the morning baby – and Ethan, thank you," Jan said, ever so quietly, as she momentarily rested her head on his shoulder.

After the day they had, some well deserve personal space was needed. At dinner, Jan and Jim sat down to have a heart-to-heart, about her irregular menstrual cycle. He encouraged her, to take a day off from university, and see their family doctor – and suggested, Ethan could go with Jan.

"Yes dad, I will do so. But it's worrying. Maybe I have cancer, or something really bad is happening to me," Jan said, in a very low and sad voice.

"Maybe none of the above, my darling. Please don't race ahead with these diagnoses. Only take one day at a time. For now, eat your dinner – and tomorrow, you will see the doctor," Jim spoke reassuringly.

He stretched his arms across the solid oak table, and touched her hand, and smiled. Jan looked at him, with so much love and respect – knowing, he had played the roles of mum and dad, so well.

"Thank you, dad. Love you," Jan replied, as she clung to Jim's hand, ever so tightly.

Jan cleared the dining table and washed the dishes. She picked up her black art case, from beside the chrome coffee table, and went to her bedroom. The door squeaks, as she shuts it. Some comfy clothes were left lying on the bed – she got changed, before laid herself down on the bed. Jan gazed at the ceiling, until she fell asleep. Next morning, Ethan's doorbell rang. Ethan got out of bed, rubbed his eyes and approached the door. He wondered, who would come by so early. He peeped through the living room window, and saw Jan. He swiftly swaddled himself in his dressing gown, and opened the door.

"Jan, is something the mattered! You look a bit pale. Come inside," Ethan, spoke hastily.

She slowly stepped inside, and stood at the door.

"I hardly slept the night through – worried something bad is happening internally. Maybe, I am dying. Today, you must go to Uni without me – I'll go and see my GP," Jan spoke, apprehensively.

Ethan looked worried, and saddened by Jan's words.

"Don't be silly, my Darling, I'll come with... You shouldn't be going on your own," Ethan empathised, in a consoling voice.

Jan kissed Ethan on his right hand, and told him to meet her at 9. He watched her walked away – then slowly shuts the door, and went back to bed.

"When it rains – it pours," Ethan, whispered to himself.

After an hour long wait at the doctor's practice, she was finally checked. The doctor concluded, Jan had imbalance hormones. This wasn't to be a huge problem, and there was nothing life-threatening. Jan was very pleased, to hear her problem wasn't huge. She was encouraged to come back for further checks, if she was still feeling worried. Jan decided to leave things, as they were. Back in the waiting room, she sat down and updated Ethan. For a moment longer, they talked about Jan's mum. Ethan was curious, about what Jan remembered. But she told him – not much. A strange lady (looked about 50s), was sitting only two seats away from Jan. She watched and listened. Suddenly she got up, and sat closer to Jan and Ethan. They stared at her for a moment…

"I will listen, if you speak," she then spoke.

Jan looked at her strangely, and asked the lady who she was.

"I was listening to your conversation, and it sounds familiar," she said.

"Last few days were really scary – and I have been thinking about my mum, lately. I can hardly remember much about her. I was so little – only five years old, when she died. But I remember her smile, it was so beautiful! She glowed, as if the sun shone in her eyes. Mum was tall, slender and very poised. Maybe I look a lot like her. I certainly have her artistic skills, and passion for fashion. However, I have seen lots of photos – and they reminded me, of the best of times we had together. I just wished, she was still here," Jan communicated her feelings about her mum – for the first time.

The lady held Jan's hand gently, and whispered, "I know… Janis died of an extreme case of diabetes, did she?"

Jan felt curious, and asked… "But eerm, I didn't tell you her name, did I?"

"She was my best friend, many years ago, before you were born… And the rest is history," the lady said.

"May I have the pleasure, of knowing your name, please?" Jan asked.

"Gloria," the lady replied.

"Your name is Jan?" Gloria asked.

"Yes… Nice to meet you Gloria – and thank you, for listening," said Jan.

Gloria, nodded her head and a smiled.

Jan and Ethan, walked slowly home. They wondered about Gloria, coincidently being at the doctors, at that time. Back at home with Jim, they went through the family album – to see photos of Janis and Gloria. But it got a bit too much for Jan, and she spoke out about the half full space, in her heart – life without her mum. She struggled more, especially when emotions are paramount. Nevertheless, Jan knew life goes on. Therefore, she pledged to complete her course, and make it to the top – and then dedicate her achievement, to her parents – especially Jim.

A year on…

Time had passed – Jan and Ethan's, hard work had paid off, and they were graduated with honours. Jan was top of her year group, and was the only student, with an overall average score of 98%. A first-class degree, was well deserved. Weeks followed, she had several job offers, and many were rejected for various reasons. However, Jan was unable to turn down, just this one. She was selected by a top fashion designing company, to join their team. An all-expense-paid opportunity, to do her masters and Doctorate – while she works with them. But it meant, Jan was going away for a while. And there were only four days, before she took off to Tokyo, Japan. Jan saw this as an amazing opportunity, to also reunite with relatives in Japan. And, although Jan was missed by her favourite men, she had their optimum supported all the way. Ethan started working, with a royal fashion designer – a dream come true. Nevertheless, he somehow knew, these opportunities came with great rewards and drawbacks. Yet, totally unprepared for precisely what they would be.

Have I told you enough, how much I love you?
Just how much, you make me feel brand new?
You filled my days with happiness,
I couldn't wish for much more,
I'm already so blessed, to have the best.
All I ever wanted my Love, is simply within you.

With you I can be me, without fear,
I can touch and hold you, in the midst of millions,
Yet, only you and I standing there.
I give you my heart freely,
Only to show, how much I care,
With you my darling, everything I will share.
Your friendship is all I need,
A place to hide my deepest secrets,
In you, I find it indeed.
I hate remembering you're so far away,
Though the thought of your love, kept me day-by-day.
But for you my darling, I will patiently wait,
Simply, because you are so great.

The only thing, I ever needed – I found in you,
I see beauty – the sort that's so rare to find,
And so, I took your delicate heart – and hid it out of sight,
A safe place in my mind.
Your entire being, is my true happiness,
And so I thank God, for giving me his finest...

CHAPTER 3

Life changes, everything changes

Jan was away for six years, though not constantly being in the same place. Surrounded by the right people, in the right places – success was at her fingertips. She was exceeding all others expectations, and excelled to the highest level. Ethan, was very proud of Jan, and didn't want to hold her back. But the distance wasn't doing them much favours – there were the occasional one to two weeks, home visits. And on a couple of occasions, Ethan had visited Jan – once in New York and another time in Milan. Jan had promised, she will be home whenever time allowed – but her goal was to succeed, in the fashion designing industry. Once her name was established, she hoped to run a fashion designing business (with the inheritance funds, given by her grandparents). However, whilst Jan's career had soared to the sky, Ethan's health plummeted to the ground – he was suffering in silence.

Ethan's health problem was ongoing for three years – but it was a secret kept from Jan. However, Jan was working in Paris – and was focusing on launching her new business. She believed, it was a great opportunity for them – as they could share the business. Being super enthusiastic, Jan got the ball rolling with the legalities. Then to ensure her launch-day is perfect, she bought Jim, Ethan and Vaisy, surprised first-class tickets to Paris. But a spanner was thrown into the works – when Ethan pulled the plug on their relationship.

Friday evening, and Jan was home from work – after a very long day. There was a letter present on the floor, just as she opened the door and walked in. Her face glowed, as Jan had recognised the handwriting. She sat down on her beautiful white, three seater sofa and read…

My Darling Jan,
   I hope life is treating you kindly. Missing you as always, it's been four months since your last visit, which had lasted a week. You know, I'm not much of a telephone person. I love seeing your beauty, rather than just hearing your voice. Maybe I'm old fashioned. But I called it love, intense attraction and romantic. I treasure everything we shared, and will for a life time. Quite often, I thought our days together weren't long enough. Before I go to bed at nights, I played the tape you left me, last time you were here. My favourite note, is when you repeatedly declared your profound love… You were unvarying, and I could feel your complete devotion. I hope you know, I was always captivated by your love, and was also completely devoted to you. As I wrote this epistle, I'm attesting this fact. Tears like a river flowing down my cheeks, but there are plenty of smiles in between.
   In reminiscing, I dream of the beauty in your eyes, it's like the morning sunlight on the horizon in Jamaica. Believe me princess, it is one of my favourite things to see. The sun that lit my world, rolled in your eyes. Never have I met anyone else, so deeply loving, caring, sensitive and understanding. You loved profoundly – beyond the limit of one's mind's eyes. When you walked into my life, all my doubts and fears vanished, and my heart was filled with **pure love***. Should I go back in time, I would stay much longer lying in your arms – and pray for those moments to last forever.*
   On my way home from work yesterday, I visited Jim. He was doing really well! Once I arrived, he instantaneously thought of lunch. Perhaps, he read my mind. My bag was off my shoulder, as I made myself worthwhile in the kitchen too. I hope you don't have a grin on your face, wondering of the disastrous meal we'd put together. Well, here's something to smile about, it was good! And while a few things packed in the oven – we did some work in the back garden. We have planted some nice red roses, just outside of your bedroom window. Removed some shrubs, and repainted the patio in duck egg blue. However, I'm sure he will give an update, next time you called.
   Unfortunately, I won't be around for much longer. I'm not quite certain, how to tell you all that I really wanted to say. Please, don't

hate me after reading this, I think it's for the best. From the deepest depth of my heart, I'm really sorry to be writing these words. I think the occasional visits, may not be necessary anymore. I'm ill, and I'm going away. By this, I meant, I will be leaving this country. I'm being diagnosed with psychosis, for three years now. I know you are thinking, why didn't I, say something sooner. It all started when I became obsessed, with the way my parents left me. One day, I went to work-out at the gym, and I had an accident. I had felt dizzy, someone came to help and I lashed out – my behaviour was out of character. I was feeling somewhat strange, and so I explained all to my GP. About a week later, I was seen by a psychiatrist, who gave my diagnosis.

I quite often experienced high and low moods, anxiety attack, lack of energy, and lost interest in my job. From time to time, I found myself sleeping more frequently, than normal – and most times, enclosed in my own world. I started smoking – surprised, I know. But the things that go on in my mind, aaaah... Only if I could physically hold them, and take them out. Then life would be a breeze. I somewhat feel as if, I don't want to be here anymore – there is no point to life. I sometimes feel angry, teary and upset – it's almost as if nothing made sense. I wondered, if I was still me – I feel trapped in my own mind. It's hard, it's really hard. However, I'm trying... I can still hear yours and Gran's voices, in my mind – reminding me of how well loved I'm. So I'm holding on to this, and I'm definitely not giving up, despite all. I'm going to fight this to the end – and stick with my treatment plan. Life is precious, and we only get one shot at it. This is why, I want you to now enjoy life – we don't know what's next... I will go away and take one day at a time, yet enjoy what I can...

I will always love you, Baby. You were the best part of my life, best friend and soul mate. I wished, we could have a life together. But should this be possible, I would only be a stumbling block in your way. So, enjoy life to its fullest – knowing that you are irreplaceable and unforgettable! No tears please! Sometimes, it's better to accept one's sacrifice, than to spend a lifetime drowning in tears and wondering thoughts. Please don't reply, I'm on my way out now – uncertain of when, I will return. Perhaps one day, life might bring us together again – but I much rather it gives us complete happiness. Please check on Gran, for me. She spoke highly of you.

E xx

Jan slowly dropped her handbag, right next to her feet, on the wooden floor. Her smile slowly went off her face. Jan became deflated, as she clenched her fists tightly on her cheeks. In the kitchen, there was a white tea-towel on her dark granite work-top. She went sluggishly, picked it up and wiped her face – before sat back down again. Jan streamed away for hours, faced down on her orange and white cushion. After a few hours of feeling weakened and alone, she gazed at the letter again, and sobbed. Suddenly, there was a heavy-handed knocking at the door, Jan scrambled her way there.

"Who is there," Jan said, in a rather low and sad tone."

"It's me – Kyle. Have you forgotten our plans for tonight?" He said, cheerfully.

"Oh no. Sorry... I meant yes," Jan replied, diffidently.

She quickly wiped her face again – and opened the door.

"Come in, please come in. Forgive me for my acute memory relapse."

Kyle, was Jan's work-mate. And had driven for over 5 miles, for them to have a night in.

"Are you feeling OK? Were you crying Jan...? You seem a bit pale," Kyle – seemingly worried.

Jan gave him the letter, and he read it through. A very understanding Kyle, went closer to Jan, held her in his arms, and gave some comfort.

"We could do this another time – or if you prefer, I could stay the night. I don't mind sleeping on the sofa," Kyle empathised, compassionately.

Jan, hung in silence for a moment.

"Just whatever suits you best, alright. I'm very sorry, you're so heartbroken Hun," said Kyle.

"Please stay, if that's OK with you. I could do with a friend," said Jan, as she side-way glanced at him.

"Sure, it's alright with me. I will leave first thing in the morning, as long as you are OK," Kyle whispered.

"Shall I put the kettle on?" Said Kyle, as he walked towards Jan's neatly compact kitchen.

Jan told Kyle, to make himself right at home. Before long, the sound of Jan's cry became even more persistent. Felt somewhat helpless, Kyle sat on the sofa next to Jan. He then held her in his arms, and whispered "Ssssh", until she cried herself to sleep. A moment later, Kyle fully rested Jan on the sofa. He thought of ways, to make Jan more comfortable – therefore he tucked her under a red-tartan-throw, which was hanging over the sofa arm. Shortly after, Kyle made a large mug of cappuccino, and a cucumber-watercress sandwich. In no time at all, he had finished eating – and was ready to turn-in for the night. Kyle's body seemed deflated, as a big yawn came out of his mouth. He slid himself off the sofa, and onto the fluffy light-brown carpet. Just before, he pulled a white knitted throw over himself. The night had gone by so quickly – it was already 10:30, he thought.

Saturday morning, Kyle woke up early. First, he used the bathroom – and left a note on the dining table (*Jan, please don't hesitate to ring, if you need a friend. X*). He then quietly sneaked out of the house, and drove home. About an hour later, Jan woke up and noticed Kyle was away. She read the note, before putting it in the kitchen bin. Jan took a shower and pulled herself together, and had just about managed to get through the morning. The house phone rang…

"Dad!" Jan softly uttered, sounded surprised.

"Yes, you were amazed that I rang?" Jim voiced, fervently.

"I was thinking of calling you, shortly. Ethan has broken up with me."

"When did this happen?" Jim asked.

"Yesterday, I came home to a letter from him. He's very ill with psychosis, and I was too caught up with my career, to even notice. Too busy to remind him, he was the love of my life. I never wanted to love any other. I didn't get the chance to make him happy, and now he's gone away."

"Maybe that's why he came to see me recently. We cooked and had a good afternoon. I didn't know… I thought he was just being considerate," said Jim, as he breathes out a big sigh.

Jim apologised intensely. Then suggested he asked Vaisy, where Ethan went. Jan told him, not to worry much. He had explained all, he wanted to say in his letter. But she will ring Vaisy at some point, as Ethan requested.

"My heart aches with pain, like never before. My chest tightened – sometimes it feels as if, someone has ripped my stomach apart. The pain spreads to my back and head rapidly – my feet are numbed. My body finally shuts down, though I am here still breathing. The pain made me angry, but feeling angrier with myself – because Ethan made me his priority, dad. And all we had worked for, suddenly broke away, like cracked ice beneath our feet – left us lonely and fragmented. He was my love, and my life."

My dear, trust that as the days go by, time will heal your broken heart. Today your wound is opened, and very sore. Living in desperation, despondency, hopelessness, and self-pity will only make it worse. Pray this experience, will count for something worthwhile. Believe, it will allow you to discover a much-improved version of yourself. A version, which will allow you to embrace life, like never before. Everyone comes into your life for a reason. Some for a longer period than others. Some may start your life's journey with you, a few may even meet you half-way, maybe just to help you to the next junction. But my dearest, it's the time you've spent with them, that mattered most. The memories that are so precious, to love and to hold on to. That's what you don't want to lose. So from now on, promise me, to make every day a special day. Don't spend too much time living in anger. By doing so, you are only hurting yourself. Ethan would like you to be happy, so try to be kinder to you – and be happy. Don't let this period, paint the rest of your life in greyness. You were his sunshine for many years, so now, you ought to shine for yourself.

Jim, took Jan on a little trip down memory lane…

"You know this story by now, but it's so good, I must share it with you again," said Jim.

"Oh dad, not yours and mum's story again."

"Yes, Darling – sure is," Jim, answered amusingly.

But listen, there is something in it for you. I never told you the full story. Janis and I met in Japan, at the Central library. She was reading a novel – *Love is love forever,* it was called. I couldn't take my eyes off her. Janis was the most beautiful Japanese I had ever met. Actually, may I rephrase that, Janis was the most beautiful woman, I had ever met. I glanced at my physical self and dreamt for a little while, wondered if this beautiful lady would like an English geezer. I got the history book, I was looking for, and then sat right next to her. I didn't hesitate too much. I thought, there was something special about her. Hence, I started discussing what I knew about Japan openly, and she joined in. I didn't need the book, after all – Janis taught me everything I knew. The conversation flowed, and we became friends from there on. I stayed there for two years, and taught English at a middle school in Tokyo (Central Japan). During that time, we fell madly in love with each other. I never looked at another woman, she was all I desired. Janis never looked at another man, I was her rock.

After an amazing time there, I had to return home. This wasn't the greatest feeling. And I was very silly. I somehow came to the most stupid idea that, it would be better for me to just leave. She was living a fantastic life – so, I thought there was no way, she would give up on her job as a professional artist, and come away with me. I had considered staying there with her, but some things needed my attention here. I pondered for months, while my heart throbbed with pain, and my mind weary of my thoughts. Even my body, felt weakened by my worries – like you are feeling, right now.

Uncertain of what to do, one morning – Sunday morning, I raced up to my friend Chingwa little house. My footsteps and my heart were in tune – to the heavy sounds, they made. Whoo, whoo, my heart beat rapidly in my chest – I don't want to hurt her, I don't want to hurt her, I chanted. I got to the top of his outside staircase, and knocked the door in quick succession. Chingwa answered curiously, as he walked towards the door – and I shouted my name.

"Come in. What's the matter...? Is someone after you?" He said, in Japanese.

I started crying – man tears ah! He took one of his sweaty T-shirts and quickly wiped my face. It wasn't the sweetest aroma! Chingwa got me to calm down, so he could understand what I was about – eventually, I explained. Chingwa got off his wooden high chair, sat on the carpet, and placed his hands on his cheeks. His motions halted, he looked at me and spoke in Japanese...

"No, you can't...! You must find a way to continue loving and protecting her. She is one of a kind. Many men here, even myself would love to be with her, and treat her like the queen she really is. But she preserved herself for years, and now love only you. Go, go now, and tell her. She will understand."

I got up slowly and went... For an instant, I made note of what to say (*My time in Japan is coming to an end, would you like to come with me please?*). Then I put the flimsy piece of paper, back into my shirt pocket. My thought was, maybe I could just give it to her, and then escaped for the day – but that was a cowardly way out. So I had to think again. A week before returning home, she had the optimum princess treatment. We did all the things, she desired... But Janis was very savvy, and missed very little.

"Something is up, please talk to me," she said, quite ardently.

And of course, I assured her not to worry – and that I loved her. At the end of the week, I left without saying a word. Well, I thought writing her a letter – once I was back home, would explain everything. And so I did. I wrote very many letters, but there was no response. Your grands were furious, I had hurt her so badly. They didn't give their consent, for us to be back together, at that time. I didn't blame them. Once bitten, twice shy, I thought.

I didn't just crush her heart, I had broken mine too. Never had I thought, one lady could have made my mind ached, so much. Everyone thought I was strong and emotionally independent. Oh, how wrong they were. My being felt like, a bird with clipped wings. My two best friends George and Andy, suggested I go back to Japan and find her – because I was no use to anyone. They thought my face was like a bewildered mask. At times, I snapped at people, who didn't deserve the bitter end of my frustration. But I wasn't coping – I then tried to think of ways, to channel my negative emotions. I had spoken with mum and dad about her, and they told me this – "love will find a way back to your heart." Wise words, I said. Not that, I thoroughly felt like it. After a heart-rending six months, life was back to normal. One day, back home from a football match, as I entered through the doors, mum shouted…

"Jimmy, is that you son? There's a letter for you. It's on the side table in the hall."

I got it, at once. Rapidly tore the flap off, sat on the mat, and read every word.

> *Hi Jimmy,*
>
> *I hope you are well. I have read all your letters, and missing you too. My life hasn't been the same, since you've been gone. Forgiveness is surely the matter here, just to let you know. Should there be a chance, you haven't been happily swept off your feet and already married, then please write back. My courage to write to you now, I hope will bring our worlds together and into focus. You're wonderful, the most sincere gentleman walked into my life, except my dad. I mentioned dad, he's still uncertain about you, at the moment. He will come around once he sees, how happy we are together again. Your ideas of romance, are all the things that ignite my lights, and lit my world brighter, than the moon and stars.*
>
> *My darling, I'm ever so appreciative of your enduring trust in me. And I hope you know, this is true – everything in my life feels perfect, when we are together. Filled, I'm filled, with the best of you, and it is simply entrancing. So my dearest, I hope we can be together again – you are simply irresistible, and I love that! Jimmy, I love you for thousands of reasons, but especially because you alight the best of my ways. You've taught me how to love, with my heart, mind and*

soul. The times we spent together, were like a dream come true. Please note, if you can still be mine, I would like to marry you. Will you take a chance on me? Awaiting your sincere response, my Love. Please don't take too long, as the distance between us is long enough.

Love xxx Mahong

"Woo-hoo!!! Happy days!!! Happy days!!!" I shouted...

Interestingly, hearing of marriage could make one think twice – and wonder if this person, will be your true destiny. I didn't wonder – I just believed... Because my entire being, was overwhelmed with love and respect, for her. In a way that, I wanted to spend every minute of my days, breathing in the air, she exhaled – and forever share our closeness, affection and absolute adoration. The energy, light and life we possessed, were at times exhilarating. Your mum, was an absolute treasure – I loved her so much. Even mum and dad could see that, I would lay my life down for her – and decided to support me all the way. So much so, in a matter of days, they invited her over to spend some time with us. It was exciting, being as she was my first proper girlfriend – the only one, I had ever introduced to my parents. We were 20 and 24 years old, as you know. But old enough to recognised, precisely what we felt for each other.

After we got married, she decided on the English name – Janis. We had you, and weren't given much of a chance to have more kids. Although Janis didn't want to have a big family. She was only from a small family of four. I wouldn't have minded, having two children. Then you would have had a sibling. However, we were grateful for what we had – our families. Your grandparents migrated and joined us here – until the day they died. Your uncle had last visited, when he came to Janis's funeral. Your mum's death was untimely, we know. But fate had brought us together, one final time. So don't fret too much, is all I wanted to say... If Ethan is your one true love – then he'll be. Get on with life, and don't stop because of a heart-break. When life decides to stop, it stops for good! There's just enough time to get over the pain – and smile again. There are things to do, people to meet and places to see – all are a part of our life experience. So, exhaust yourself with joy, and go find your path to happiness – it awaits your feet. Troubles are stepping stones, to our next big adventure.

My love left me, suddenly I feel as if there's no hope,
My mind tightens, like a twisted rope,
My lungs struggle, I could hardly breathe,
As a sudden gush of guilt, ripped through me.
I'm feeling so ill, my stomach churns,
Weakened and helpless, I am,
My body hurts, whichever way I turn.
I pray for us to be alright, once more,
As I hate remembering, you were my best friend,
The one, I shared my whole world with,
And now, all we had come to an abrupt end.

I see the traits my heart desire, in you,
They are beautiful,
And I just want to say, I love you.
In my heart is a secure home,
I would like to make it just your own.
Oh, how beautiful, we would be,
Afloat in the air triumphantly,
Only if you could see the best in me,
And simply let us be.

CHAPTER 4

The pain no one else sees

No deep-cut wound, is ever healed in a day – hence, Jan continued with her normal work routine, despite the weight her heart was carrying... A week later, whilst Jan was on her lunch break, she rang Vaisy.

"Helloo," Vaisy, answered the house phone after two rings.

"Hi Granny V, its Jan," she said, in a polite and slightly raised voice.

"Oh, hello Jan!" Vaisy responded, sounding somewhat surprised.

"How are you? Is everything going alright?" Jan asked, sympathetically.

"I'm doing alright, my love. Considering my boy is away," Vaisy answered.

"Sad... Isn't it?" Jan said, with a lower tone.

"So, GV, have you managed to talk to Ethan, since...?" Jan asked.

"Yes, yes. Oh sure! Ethan calls every day. Sometimes two or three times a day. Just knowing he's OK and striving well, kept me going. He's my preciousness, but you already know that Hunny," Vaisy spoke, with cheerfully.

"Are you keeping well?" Vaisy asked Jan, sounded a little concerned.

"Yes, thank you. Ee, Erm – sorry, no need pretending to you GV. Actually, I'm merely trying to face each day. Work kept me busy, until I'm alone."

"I understand... I know, my dearest," Vaisy replied.

"Do you think, I should go after him? I still want us to be together, Granny V – I want this more than anything. I wished he had given me the chance, to reply to his letter. Ethan is all I wanted in a partner, a soul-mate, a husband. Only we didn't get the chance to be engaged – I felt robbed. How could he do this to us? I-I would have come back home to him, if he had given me the opportunity to do so. I loved him, I still do."

Vaisy, listened and sighed.

"Wish I could help – but I can't! Ethan had sworn me to secrecy. I must respect his request. Perhaps, you should too. Please don't take this the wrong way, my dearest Jan. You know, I love you like a granddaughter." Said Vaisy, in a low and apologetic voice.

Suddenly, Jan heard a grunting sound from Vaisy, she sounded unwell. Are you well?" Jan swiftly asked.

"Yeah… Yes, I am alright. But I must go now. Please don't be a stranger, when you come to visit," Vaisy, quickly dismissed the conversation and said bye.

"Bye GV, I will call you again soon," Jan whispered quietly, as the phone beeped.

Jan wasn't convinced, everything was alright. She hoped if there was a problem, Vaisy would call someone nearby to assist. Jan hated knowing, Vaisy was on her own at age 85. And without frequent visits, from loved ones. A little later, Jan was still feeling perturbed about Vaisy's abrupt end, to their phone conversation. She thought of asking Jim to check on Vaisy, but didn't want to worry him, in case it was nothing. So, she rang back instead. First, there was no answer. Jan rang again, and Vaisy answered.

"Hello, hello, sorry – now is not a good time to talk!" Vaisy, sounded on edge.

Jan stayed silent for a little while. Then said, "Ganny V, it's me again – I'm very worried about you, will you please, talk with me for a minute? At least, put my mind at ease."

Another pause, as they hung in silence. Jan had a feeling, Vaisy wasn't paying her any mind.

"What's the weather like there today? If it's a really lovely day, maybe I could ask my dad to come around and visit you… Perhaps, he could put on a barbecue," Jan, spoke insistently.

"No, I'm fine. I will be alright. Maybe I could talk with you, but I don't want to take much of your time. And promise me, you won't feel like I'm your burden."

"Oooh Granny V… I love you, like I had loved my own Grans. So please, don't ever feel this way," Jan swiftly responded.

Vaisy expressed her feelings to Jan. I understand, Ethan reasons for leaving. But I'm ever so worried. And every now and again, my head hurts really badly – it started after Ethan left. He struggles massively, with his mental illness – but, so do I. On a daily basis, I watched him, a little bit of my beautiful grandson chipped away, into a cocoon. Sometimes, I wonder how much of the real Ethan, will remain. The highs and lows of his condition, left us feeling despair and helpless – but I always give a listening ear. Although, I am experiencing all this first hand, I don't think I could ever totally understand, what he must be feeling. She paused... Sound of sobs...

"Are you OK GV, it sounds as if you were crying? I'm here for you alright. Take your time," Jan said, softly and sympathetically.

"That's enough said," Vaisy whispered, in a whimpering and sad sounding voice.

Jan was very kind, and told her, she could make more time to listen... She wasn't expected back at work for a while. Vaisy continued.

"OK, then. Please hold on for sec... I need a comfy cushion, for my back." She picked up the green floral one, from beside her posh fabric sofa, Ethan had bought her.

"Are you still there?" Vaisy said.

"Yes, I am... In your own time GV," Jan replied.

"Erm, where was I? Oh, right – eerm," Vaisy muttered.

There were days, I watched him feeling emotionally trapped, frustrated and confused. Quickened away, when there is an anxiety attack. Melted down to floor level, though not quite literally. Medications were his saviour, most times. And, if he missed them for a day, or even changed dosages; he could be in for a real roller coaster ride. Never have I seen him, so possessed with paranoia and delusion. His delusions were incredibly difficult for him to cope with. Out of nowhere, he would voice the most unrealistic thoughts. Ethan would even questioned why, he had heard sounds and voices, no one else has heard. A common question was, you are not going to leave me – aren't you, Gran? I thought, you said you are leaving me – just like my parents did. But was this my grandson, Oliver (his grandfather) and I brought up together, until the day he passed away? I have been on my own with Ethan since then. There shouldn't be any doubt in his mind. But I also understand, his thought-processing may have been severely disturbed. No matter how tedious his journey becomes, I will be there for him, until the day of my passing. I am the only constant person, in his life.

Ethan's condition was exhausting – many nights, he struggled to sleep because his nightmares were deep and constant. He experienced night terrors, which made him believe people were out to get him. In these moments, Ethan screamed terrifyingly, as he struggled to wake up. And Instead of braving it back to bed, he turned to alcohol – and become addicted. As a result, he suffers from epileptic seizures, high blood pressure, slight memory loss and coordination difficulties. I was terrified, he would have mouth/throat cancer, and even liver cirrhosis. Even frightened of what could happen to him, when he was out drinking. The chances of him getting robbed, beaten and killed. One day, he crashed emotionally – Ethan drank so much, his psychosis manifested and caused him to hallucinate. Suicidal and self-harming, came into the picture too. This was one of the many times, he was rushed to hospital – and was admitted for eight months. I thought, this would be his turning point. But it wasn't! He just made empty promises, for my peace of mind.

Nonetheless, it didn't take much pressure, for him to confess to his doctor – he was never off alcohol. It wasn't a behaviour I could totally understand – especially, when it resulted in him being ill, unconscious and extremely tired. All the positive things, he used to do – was suddenly no more... And everything that came out of his mouth was either lies, or absolutely negative. Also, he traded one addiction for another, so he did it all. Drugs when he was a teenager, after his gramps died, and now all this. Selfish and tunnel-minded – yet a cry for help, I know. For a while, he's been ill without any realisation – it must have been awful. Frustration was the epitome, of his days. I supposed acceptance, is key. He is now finding it easier, to put his feelings into context. In recent days, he seems less stressed, less fearful and no very confused.

Prior to his diagnosis, I used to watch him doubted me for so long, he had become blinded to the amazing gran, I am. I have listened to the things he had said about me, speaking to his psychiatrist. They were unbelievable horrible! It felt as if, I was the devil, who haunted his life. However, his diagnoses brought out my forgiveness – whole-heartedly. My stomach-pit churned, as I spoke about it all. Still, I live in fear, uncertain of how he will be tomorrow. Will he do something stupid? Will he somehow have an inclination that, life can be sweeter tomorrow than today? I pray, Ethan will remember the happy fun-loving boy, inside him. I know beneath his condition, is my beloved grandson... Just the most amazing person ever! The one, I'm most proud of. I hope he has always known, my heart housed all the love, I could ever give him. For Ethan, my love is always the strongest.

Never have I experienced anything, so petrifying – considering my golden age. These days, have exposed my weakest moments, in time. I am no longer, young and strong with good emotional resilience. So I wasn't equipped with the required knowledge, to deal with Ethan's personality transplant – and his many different sides. I was weary of his sad and deflated face, hanging towards his knees – as his emotional pain surfaced. He went from normal, to the obsessive addict, who cherished the gravest thought – suicide! Oh, how sad? My heart bleeds incessantly. Occasionally, I felt absolutely numbed, by the horror in his voice. Seldomly, I want to exchange places with him. So I could die happy, knowing I gave him hope – and he could finally be at peace. Still, I took it all in my stride, and did everything, I could – included paid thousands of pounds from my pension, for the best private care and support. Hoping I could still be his rock, and saved him from watching his life slowly disappear, like water vapour.

I wish for Ethan, to find himself – and live a happy life. Ethan was lost, since he was born. I had found him – and I hope, I won't lose him again. I don't think he had ever really known, who he was. But a brilliant young man, Ethan was before his diagnosis. He behaved in such a respectable manner, which reflected good social standing. I wished things had worked out for both of you, Jan. Maybe I really should tell you, where he went – although he might not be there. He went to Jamaica to find his mother and father. Then he will be travelling to Mexico, his father's homeland to meet extended families. Maybe one day, he will be back. But if there are questions, needed answering – and he wants to find his roots, then my blessings go with him.

You are very kind and considerate, my darling. Thank you, sweetheart. But I really think, you should go now, my love. I have got Tilly to talk with, if I need to talk more. She will stop by – I won't ever get lonely. Erm, you know Tilly, she never shuts up – not even when she's sleeping. Even then her mouth constantly, opens and shuts.

"OK, Granny V, I will go now. Promise you will call me or dad, if we can be of any help, at any time. Maybe Tilly could sleep over some nights, she's a bit lonely too."

"Yes, I will. Bye for now, then love."

"Bye GV," Jan softly replied.

Jan was left feeling extremely emotional, guilty and broken all over again. She spent another 25 minutes, sat on the toilet seat and wept. Jan was very distressed, as there was so much she didn't know about Ethan.

She thought it was unimaginable, what he went through on his own. Even more so, he courageously took his journey one day at a time. Regardless of the extremity of Ethan's condition, Jan wished she had the opportunity, to be there and supported him the whole way. She would have even travelled the world with him, if he wishes. There was simply no limit. Jan felt a great depth of concerned for Ethan, being away in foreign countries, without familiar faces and support. No one with a shoulder for him to cry on… Or some warm arms to hold him tight. No one to say, it will be alright. No one, to accompany him to the doctors. But she hoped, the time they spent together – and the love they shared will be sufficient to carry him through.

"My job was always important to me, but I missed the mark with Ethan. We communicated quite frequently. Although it now seems, we never really talk about the things, which were more imperative. Had I known how things were, I would have given up my job for him, and be there until… I wanted to tell the world, Ethan isn't just a man – he was my special someone, my best friend, and a heartbeat that's now missing…"

My tear drops turned into blood,
The day, I found out you are so broken,
Lost and confused, I am,
My heart too, was cut open.
Slashed with sharp lies,
And deeply wounded with despair,
Still, I wonder why,
My love wasn't enough to protect you?
And keep you soaring high?
But my darling, for you,
My infinite love unceasingly flows.

CHAPTER 5

Decision making

Jan had endured, a right-lonesome two years. Seemingly, most guys had felt intimidated by her beauty, and didn't pluck-up the courage to ask her out. However, Jan was not interested in having an intimate relationship – or even remotely tempted by the very sleek, handsome and mouth-wateringly, gorgeous models. But it was only a matter of time, before her jaws were dropped – when she met the very sweet, charming and sensitive Italian stunner, Marcello Mendez. The only one, to totally captured Jan's attention. He was a high profile fashion designer – who had just been employed by the company, Jan was working with. Marcello had the image of a Greek God. He was a younger and sexier version of Hercules – the epitome of perfection! The tone of his voice was to die for... Just through pure utterance, Marcello could have any lady kissing his feet, never mind his gorgeous lips. And being multilingual, he was a definite an eye-catcher.

One morning, Jan went to work and found a note on her desk – (*My Lady Jan, could I interest you in having lunch with me, please? MM*). Jan was flattered, as she funnily whispered to herself "MM – must mean Mystery Man." Though, she knew it was Marcello's initials. Jan did not respond to his first invitation. She felt a bit uncertain about him – since ladies were flocking him, like sheep to a pasture. Marcello was insistent – and made a second attempt, two days later. Jan was on her way back from a work conference, when she saw him entered her unlocked office. He searched for her work diary, and placed a note inside. Jan snuck behind Marcello and gave him a fright. "Busted!" Marcello said softly, as he tried to explain with a slight stutter. Marcello told Jan, he would like if the answer was yes. Distracted by his sexy physique, Jan momentarily dreamt of squeezing Marcello's bum cheeks. But surely, this wasn't ladylike – for Lady-Jan! So of course, she tamed her wild thought. Marcello gave Jan a soft gaze, before gracefully walked away. Still, Jan was God-smacked, and somewhat quite amused. As Jan sat at her desk, she read the note – (*One date please? MM*).

Jan was impressed with his insistence. She took a little wander over to his workroom, just five doors, to the left of her office. Making a habit of sneaking-up on Marcello – Jan walked in quietly, and stood next to his ladies' evening wear designs. She light-handedly stroked a long mint-green, satin dress – hung on the long metal clothes rail. Then softly cleared her throat, eeeh eem! Marcello finally noticed he wasn't alone, and walked away from the wide glass windows, overlooked the busy streets below.

"Um, sorry for breaking into your office, and left that note… Not sure, what I was thinking."

Marcello, stood in silence for a while. Jan took the initiative to talk about his flawless designs. Something everyone had praised him for. His face lit up, like a torch in the heavens. Marcello smiled at Jan for the first time, since she walked in the room. Jan slowly walked closer, and stood next to him. Silence, pure silence for a few more minutes.

"Wouldn't you like to ask me in person? Maybe, I would like the sound of your voice better, than our prominent silence," Jan spoke teasingly.

Marcello had that expression on his face – that says sorry, please forgive me, I'm an idiot! Jan walked away, and exited his workroom – through the door, led to the long stretched corridor.

"Say you will come out with me, on a date – Em please?" Marcello, finally spoke.

Before Jan could respond, Marcello presumed he knew what she would say. He looked straight into her eyes, then hung his head low. His facial expression said it all – a thought, he hadn't just embarrassed himself. Jan turned around slowly, and told Marcello, she thought he would have never asked. She re-entered the room, and requested he asked her again in Italian.

"Vi prego di uscire con me su una data."

Big smiles across their faces. Marcello felt elevated – a glimpse of hope he thought.

Jan looked at him flirtatiously, as she twirled her slim body, and softly said, "Grazie per avermelo chiesto. Devo controllare il mio diario e dirvi quando sto vicino?" "Thank you for asking. Shall I check my diary, and maybe we could fix a date then?"

"Yes please, Miss Jan Macbeth," Marcello said, rather professionally – with big smiles spread across his face.

As Jan walked away, she thought – so, the cat hasn't got your tongue after all, Marcello. However, she felt a little dubious, whether this was what she really wanted. Yet, she stifled her most genuine feelings, and went with compulsion. Surely, she had given some thoughts to moving on – and create a new chapter of her life. Perhaps one that would be lighter, and fun-filled.

Shortly after Jan got back to her office, the telephone rang. Her heart rapidly skipped a beat – as there was another thought of Ethan.

"You are through to Jan Macbeth," she answered.

There was a fuzzy sound through the phone line. Then finally a voice, "Hello, hello Jan, its dad. Are you there?"

"Dad, she exclaimed softly, are you alright..? You wouldn't normally call my work phone. You got me worried there. Is everything alright?"

"It's Ethan, he is back! I saw him at the corner shop this morning," Jim spoke, quite swiftly.

"This morning…? Are you sure about that dad?" Jan asked.

"Yes, I am. Ethan was getting a few things for Vaisy. He bought her some snacks, juices, garden magazines and mint sweets," Jim replied.

"They are a few of her favourite things," Jan said, in a slow speech.

"We spoke, but briefly. Apparently, there was a breaking at Vaisy's house, three nights ago –and he is back after being told of the news."

"A breaking? What happened? Was she hurt? Did they take anything precious from her?"

"Not much. She struggled with one guy, who tried to break into her safety box – where she had some money and precious jewelries. But instead, Vaisy did a clever thing – she freely handed him a leather bag, which was kept next to the safety box. She told him all her treasures were in it, and a few thousand pounds. But it was just a big bag, with dozens of dirty knickers – she had stored up over the years. Apparently, it was always there, just in case this day had come." Jim replied.

"Oh dear, dad! She must be shaken-up. I would be in pieces, if that was you," Jan spoke, with a great depth of worry in her voice.

"I know love. But don't worry too much. Things might have settled down now, I went and visited her this afternoon, at the hospital. Vaisy has a broken ankle, as a result of her struggles with the burglar," Jim responded.

"Did Ethan ask for me, dad?"

But before Jim answered Jan's last question, he stressed, how very sad and unfortunate for an old lady to be robbed. And suggested, Vaisy's family ought to be thinking about, getting someone to live with her. He kept talking, while Jan was still waiting for an answer. Jim suddenly remembered to answer Jan's question.

"Ethan and I, mentioned you briefly in conversation. But he didn't ask much about you. He seemed eager to get on with his day."

"I must go, dad. I don't think, I can work today. I will request the rest of today off, and take a breather," said Jan.

"I love you, dad – and thanks for calling," Jan repeated twice.

Jan told Marcello something came up, that needed her urgent attention back in England. They both hoped, all will be alright. But a disappointed Marcello, trusted Jan will return soon, for their date. She had requested time off work, effective immediately. They understood, it was something important – although she didn't tell them, the whole story. Jan went home, booked her flight – and travelled back to the UK next day. This was her opportunity to get closure. Considering, Ethan might not be back for good. The house phone rang, it was Kyle. He heard of Jan's leaving, from a work colleague. Jan explained all – and asked him kindly, to keep an eye on her rented apartment. She told Kyle, the key will be inside a swede, just by her front door. He encouraged Jan to be strong, and reminded her to call on him, anytime.

Next day, Jan was back in the UK on a surprise visit. First, she stopped by Ethan and Vaisy's home. She paid the cab driver £20 extra – and then asked him to drop off her bags by Jim.

"Erm, ma'am, maam – this is too much, just £25, said the driver."

"Considered lunch, on me today," Jan anxiously replied.

The driver drove away – while Jan let herself through the opened gate, before slowly knocked on Vaisy's front door. The sound of a familiar walking, was heard – when suddenly, she felt as if all her heart's shattered pieces, were magnetically pulling together. Ethan opened the door...

"Ja-Jan! You are here? What are you doing here? Ji-Jim told you?" He said, in a surprise and hesitant voice.

"Yes, dad told me. I had to come straight away – well, next day."

"Can I come in?" Jan asked.

"Erm... No. Yes, yes. Of course, it's lovely seeing you," Ethan said, as he lowered his gaze.

"Which is it, yes or no?" Jan asked.

"Um, yes. But I didn't expect you today," Ethan replied.

Jan felt a bit suspicious. Despite the surprise, she wasn't greeted with a hug.

"No – you weren't expecting me at all," Jan responded.

"How is Granny V?" Jan asked, as she eye-scanned the living room.

"Gran is doing OK, thanks – she's still in hospital. Other health issues came to light, so she's getting checked over. But we really should catch up, a bit later. Possibly back at yours, if you don't mind, please," Ethan sounded a bit hasty.

A hesitant Jan, decided she was going nowhere, until Ethan talked with her. It was obvious, he was hiding something significant. This wasn't just about his grand's incident. About ten minutes later, Jan heard some sounds coming through from upstairs.

"What's that sound Ethan, did you hear it? Is someone else here with you?"

"There are some things I need to tell you, but you must bear with me, please. Erm, would you like a cuppa?" Ethan asked.

"Yes, please. Thanks you," Jan replied.

"Why you are acting so strangely?" She asked.

"I spent several months wondering about you. Feeling upset and guilty for not being here. Tired my mind out with weariness, just hoping you were safe and happy," Jan voiced, with tears flowing down her cheeks.

Ethan was finally touched by Jan's emotions. He slowly went closer to Jan, hugged really tight and kissed her, just a little smack on her neck and lips. Quite instantly, Jan felt something was indeed different about him. Ethan caressed her hands, as he decided to be open and honest. But before the conversation got deeper – Jan rang Jim, and let him know she will be home later. She asked Jim, if the taxi driver had dropped off her suitcase. Jim told her no, and that he was at home all day. Jim was just about to get upset – but Jan told Jim not to worry, she will let it go. Jan was more worried about Ethan.

"Oatmeal biscuits and tea, at the ready," Ethan shouted.

They sat on the oak wooden chair, in the back conservatory. For the first time, Jan saw a little of the old Ethan again. She observed him keenly, and noticed despite the changes, he still had feelings for her.

Ethan took Jan's hands, and placed them on his thighs – before explained that, his letter to her was from a good place. Jan was about to speak, but Ethan puts his right index finger on her lips, and softly whispered…

"Shsss – I really got to tell you all, and we don't have much time. You will understand why in a moment. My condition has me confined, to medications and frequent health checks. There are aspects of my life that, I don't want to subject you to anymore. I love you too much. I must allow you to have the best life you can. Your most unfortunate days will be great days, in comparison to a good day with me. I felt changed – not sure how much of this new person, is the Ethan you had always known. Happiness is key, and don't you ever forget that."

Ethan explained, more in depth that, he went away to find himself. And also to find answers, to years of unanswered questions. To see if he could find away, through his life's maze – that trapped him in. He didn't accomplish all his missions. Nevertheless, Ethan had sufficient important information, to let him move on with the rest of his life. Several family members and friends, have helped him to find his parents. When he finally found where there were living, they didn't open the door. He had spoken to them through the letter box, of their one-bedroom wooden house. Ethan sat outside at the front of their house, and waited for an hour. During this time, they wrote him a letter. Jan looked at him, with so much love and empathy. She clung to his fingers, and placed each of her own between his, as she read the letter.

Dear Son,

We had always known a day would come, when you would find us. Though shocked that today is the day. First of all, we can see that you are well. We must apologise earnestly, for the way we have treated you. Now, you are so such a handsome young man – all grown up. Your auntie Gilly, have sent us some photos of you, and told us about your progress. Mum must have updated her.

We never felt anything less than love for you, but we are deeply ashamed of our doings in your life. We must live with it. I know, we will never be able to forgive ourselves for such a mistake. Nothing can bring back those years, we have missed out of your life. The best things money can't buy. And nothing can be in exchanged for it. Your first smile... First word... First step... First school... The days you cried for aches and pain, and we weren't there to give you comfort. To tell you, it will be alright. To answer doubtful questions, to kiss, hug, hold, play and most importantly, to see the best of you in action. To be whom we were supposed to be, your mum and dad. Who would really want to miss out, on life's most beautiful experience? If everyone knows, the importance of raising their kids, despite challenging, there would be many more happy people.

The day you were born, was the best and worst day of our lives. An angel was born, and you were ours. But we didn't love you enough, to put you first. So today onwards, you should always put yourself first, without feeling guilty and live your life without us. We don't deserve you. Back in the day, our hearts were filled with selfishness, and guilt. And still is today, but it's more to do with us feeling ashamed... It was totally heartless. Mum had done such a great job! We knew she would, and that's the reason you were left in her care. In case you have any question, which you would like to ask us – these two, we can answer right now. You are our only child, we couldn't face having another, after the scars we have given you. We are broken, and poor as a church mouse – but wouldn't want to accept anything from you. We don't earn much, but we get by. However, enclosed is a small saving we have, please accept it for the cost of your hotel ($US100), and a recent photo of me and your dad.

Don't come back, we can't see you again. Mum is your mother. She is proud of you – likewise, you should be very proud of yourself. We have no right, to ask you any favour. But if you will, could you kindly give mum my love, please? I missed her a great deal, but she also doesn't deserve us. Her life was much better without my troubles. Mum and dad, had three of us (Gilly, Jamie and me), they looked after us, all through their troubles.

So, I am a fulltime idiot! We would like to say hugs and kisses, but wouldn't want to be so impertinent. I think mum earned that honour, a million times more. However, some of our relatives, live only a few houses away to your right – as you exit our place. My brother (Jamie) and family. They would be pleased to meet you, if you would like to visit. It's the big blue and red house, with the electric gates. Be careful, there are loose dogs – and they don't take too kindly to strangers. You didn't have to know this, but it's the least we can do. I could write forever, as there's so much to say... I bet, you've got much more to share, than we have. And, rightly so. Don't drop a tear over us, all you are, is much greater than we'll ever be.

Annetta & Buremitto

Ethan took the letter, sat on the green grass outside and read it, while he streamed away. They watched from the side of their narrow glass windows. He could sense that, they were taking it all in. Ethan looked at the window, and saw them looking back at him. He suddenly thought, he resembled his dad, despite having a few facial features of his mum. Without hesitation, Ethan took his pen out of his brown shoulder bag, and wrote on the back of the letter they gave him.

If I broke your window, would you come out? Anyway, don't be scared, I really wouldn't break it – I'm too broken to break anything. You were right about all that you've said. Indeed, you are cowards and don't deserve our love. But today I got closure. Oh... Hello... I hoped I have said that, first thing today? It's now time to say goodbye. That's all you both managed to say to me at birth, and once again, another chance to say those precious and common words. Here I am, thinking that you were feeling sorry. But you can't even afford to make it right. I will be thankful for the opportunity, shall I? I'm really... Hello again, and goodbye!

Ethan puts it through the letter box, and then walked towards an open lot, about 10 feet away. This was in the opposite direction, to where his relatives lived. He took a moment to breathe, and eye-scanned the place. After an instant, Ethan remembered, he still had the money they gave him. So he walked back, and put it through the letter box. Ethan spoke to them, from the other side of the door, "I'm booked into a hotel, and my bills are paid." The gate opened, a little girl about 11 years old, walked through.

"Who are you?" She said.

"I'm Ethan – Ethan Sohares," he replied, with a glimpse of smiles on his face.

"Okay, I'm just here to see my auntie. Does she know you are here...?" She asked politely.

"Yes, but I was just leaving. Maybe I'll see you again, sometime," Ethan affably, responded – as he lowered his gaze and walked away.

Seeing his cousin, made him more curious to meet the rest of the family. And so, Ethan went and met his relatives. They were very pleased to see him. Everyone was alerted, and they had a welcome lunch in his honour.

Annetta and Buremitto were invited, but they didn't turn up, until just before Ethan left. Ethan, saw them approached the gate – and shamefully stood there for about 10 minutes. He went outside to meet them. They saw him stood about three feet away, and finally decided to put their selfishness aside. Straight over to where he was standing, they went. Hugged him ever so tightly, and kissed his cheeks several times – before breaking down in tears. They could hardly speak. Everyone stood back and watched – and allowed them to have a moment. A day of mixed emotions. After that, they all went home. Ethan, went back to his hotel and took it all in. His family invited him to stay, but he politely asked for his space.

Next, he went on another family adventure. This time – Mexico, where he had spent most of his time. He said it was less emotional – but was just as delightful!

And ooh, those noises that sounded from upstairs, were some professional packers. Ethan had found Vaisy's will – she left him everything. Therefore, he had sold the house without Vaisy's knowledge. And planned to let her know, on the day she got released from hospital. Furthermore, the doctors had confirmed Vaisy had high blood pressure. From there on, Ethan was determined to look after his grand – come what may... With or without help and support, from their family.

After Vaisy was released, they stayed at Jan and Jim's home for a little while, until some things were sorted. Once again, Jan pushed for a relationship with Ethan – she begged him, to let it be. Ethan in turn, had given Jan a few choices – but ones which were so difficult, she was no further forward. First, he suggested both of them could run away together, and leave Vaisy with Jim – until they got settled somewhere. Second, they could all go away together – fresh start. However, there should be no concrete plans. And finally, Jan could just give-up on trying to make it work – and enjoy life her way. Ethan explained, it was hard enough to look after himself – because some days, the weight of life felt heavier, than it really was. Other days, he felt like a volcano was inside his head – and it would erupt without notice. Then build up again like a cycle of explosions, which may not go away.

"This isn't the life you deserved. Please my darling, just let me remember your love, each day I tried to live. Though, you may be free... Free from what I'm bound by. I would like to feel mentally free, but I may never be," Ethan expressed his emotions.

They hugged, kissed and got carried away – one last night of passion, which was blissful. It was the best and worst – as they knew this was the end. Perhaps, it was one of the hardest things, they had ever done. Knowing, they had to say good-bye the next day. This time, Jan didn't want to know, where they would be living. Then she would again, want to find him.

Ethan had hired a removal van, to take most of their things to a storage unit nearby. They were going to stay at a bed and breakfast, a week before their rented house was ready. Jan offered to at least drive them there. On their way, just around the deadly deep curve, a male hit-and-run driver, had crashed into Jim's car. It was overturned. People nearby had seen the accident, and called the ambulance. A strong sense of darkness filled the air, as everyone at the scene felt gloomed. The paramedics worked fast, and as quick as they could, they were at the nearest hospital. Vaisy had a heart attack, Ethan had a head injury, and Jan miraculously escaped, with minor cuts and bruises all over her body. Jan was released from hospital, the same day. Next day, she went back to check on Ethan and Vaisy – and they weren't OK. But there was nothing, she could do to help. Jan hugged them delicately, and kissed them goodbye – though, how sad it was for them all. Jan had blamed herself for the accident – but at least this time, she was there with Ethan and Vaisy.

Jim was left once more, to pick up the pieces, and consoled Jan for many months. Jan was uncertain how to live, with such memory – it was the ultimate struggle. They returned to Paris for nearly 3 years – a long break. And also to tie up some loose ends – and then, back to the UK. On their return home, they bumped into Gloria. She told them, Ethan hadn't recovered from his injury. And was therefore, relocated to a neurological facility, elsewhere. Ethan's parents agreed to take him back, once he was allowed to be home. Vaisy, sadly didn't make it. She had another heart attack, and unstoppable internal bleeding. Vaisy's children, grandchildren and friends, came and gave her a good farewell.

In more than one way, Jan had a few endings of her own. It was the end of her and Marcello, and they didn't even get started. Jan decided to make some huge changes in hers and Jim's lives – as she urged him for a permanent change. He agreed – and sold their house. Jim had bought a lovely two bedroom bungalow, and a new silver convertible car. Whilst Jan had bought her first home, next door Sandy. After all was said and done, Jan acknowledged that, family is one of the most important things in life.

"Losing Ethan, helped me to acknowledge my mistakes. My career means a lot, but if I lose my job, I will start again. If I lose my dad, my whole world would crumble. So now, dad and I are living in close proximity – and I have launched my own business. And you Sandy, you're just fab, best friend ever! I am thankful to God for everything," Jan spoke appreciatively.

So, finally landed. Since then, Jan hasn't had another boyfriend. She did many things... Focused on her career... Devoted time to herself and Jim, as he was all the family she had around.

"Today is the day then, I promise to always remember Ethan – but I will move on from my past, accept my present, and look forward to finding my future Mr Right," said Jan.

"One day, a good and honest man, will make you a happy wife," Sandy thoughtfully communicated to Jan.

Jan was happy to hear those words, and wished the same for Sandy – as they hugged in the name of sisterhood. Sandy was amazed, no one could tell Jan had such weight, on her shoulders.

"Well, it must be your lucky day. I availed myself to listen patiently. But glad we did!" Sandy, voiced cheerfully.

"Thank you, Hun. I'm glad you could listen. I hadn't opened up this much before. But from now on, nothing is hidden from you," said Jan.

"Alright, I am holding you to that Missy," Sandy replied, with a chuckle.

Sandy assured Jan once again, it was OK. And, it was a good session for her too. Although there were moments, when Sandy closed her eyes, and tranced away at the sound of Jan's voice.

"Let's spend some time at the fountain ring, only 20 minutes away – and we could check out the spa. Besides, the change of scenery would do us a great deal of good," Sandy suggested.

At the fountain ring Jan asked Sandy, if she didn't want to find that special someone. Sandy told her, she wasn't ready for another relationship. She was happy being single.

"My past experience with men is very colourful. Next time around, I would like to find the right one for me, and stick with him. Perhaps, I should say, one who will stand by me and become my world. My relationships always started well, and ended up really bad – like really bad! I was always getting dumped by men, mistreated, misunderstood and misguided. My life, my mind and my body, got quite used to these three words, Jan, USED, REFUSED AND ABUSED. So these days, I'm taking it easy and enjoying an uncomplicated life."

Jan was keen to find out, if Sandy had a particular type of man in mind – for the future. Sandy expressed, a nice Welsh man would do. And maybe they could speak Welsh, when making love.

"Spill, spill all – you can't soak up my six pints of tears, if I can't be your rock. So, I want to hear everything," Jan voiced, enthusiastically.

"Well, we must get the hankies out then – there will be some real tear Jerker moments. We might even create, our own water well here today," Sandy spoke jokily.

My parents are Welsh as you know, from a very working class background. But I didn't always listen to what I'm being told. So my life was in my hands, particularly where boys were concerned. Though, I don't often boast about my beauty, I used it to my advantage. And allowed others to use me for their benefit. I thought my beautiful blue eyes, plumped lips perfectly proportioned, gorgeous mid-length blond hair, my size eight slim built body, was all I needed to take me through life. Even though, I'm only 5ft 6. Everywhere I went, people were always amazed by my beauty. Boys were continuously, dribbling over me. I knew it... I saw it... I felt it. And, so I thrived on it. In a nutshell, I was a tear-away – and I did it all for boys! Attention and sex, were a part of it too. My parents had always showed me love, my siblings were great and supportive. They had encouraged me to change my lifestyle. But I didn't – back in those days. I knew about protecting myself, from sexually transmitted diseases. Yet, I didn't always do a great job at it. You can say how silly, was I...

I was only 14, and lived with my ex-boyfriend, who was 39. One day, I had suddenly felt very ill, and didn't know what was wrong. And Instead of helping, he threw me out... I was left on the street, in the middle of winter. After that time, I was with any man, who could give me a place to sleep. But none of them, had showed me love. One man, had beaten me so badly, I was left with broken cheekbones. Another, threw me to the ground, twisted my ankle and broke my left arm – because I was too ill, to perform for him. I was just a tool, to be used. If each of them was a coloured marker, my body would have been the perfect reflection, of a colour circus.

Many days, I was hungry, weaken, stunk and dirty. I survived on people's refuse – that was my life. And so, there came a moment when I decided, I am a disgrace to the human race, and more so to my family. They didn't deserve my representation. Many people on the streets, were begging food and money. I was dying of hunger, but asked for only one thing, a lift to the hospital from a taxi driver. He asked me what was my story, and I told him all. He turned and looked at me in scorned – and I didn't blame him. I would scorn myself back then too, if I could. Nevertheless, he took me to the hospital – and asked for nothing in return. And that was one of the best favours, ever granted to me! And I will always be grateful, for that moment in time. I spoke to the doctor about my situation, and he didn't hesitate to assure my safety and comfort.

"Well, you won't be leaving the hospital for a very long time, Miss Sandy Dowell. So get some rest, while we take care of you," the doctor, had bossily ordered.

I laid myself on the bed and reflected, I thought – my three older siblings, were doing amazingly well. They had great careers too, and most certainly weren't abused by anyone. Despite their own upheavals, they embraced life as it should be. But this was because, they listened and humbly accepted good guidance from our parents. Whereas, I didn't! No one was to be blamed, for the decisions I made. And so, I was totally responsible for all the pain – I inflicted upon myself. So, that was my turning point.

The doctor and I fell in love, I know he also took advantage, as I was still a young girl. And he was in his late 20's. However, he was very encouraging and supportive. We lived together, and he got me a cleaning job at the hospital – under false pretence, that I was 18. From there on, we had put our finances together, so that I could further my studies. And without a fuss or a frown, he was there for me, all the way. Despite a few down times, we had lots of fun. Especially, when we played doctor and nurse behind the curtains, next to the mortuary – it was usually very quiet there. Ohw, those were the days! The best days! Filled with laughter and excitement. But sadly, we broke up seven years later, because he went back to Malaysia, and opened his own medical practice. It was his lifelong dream. He had asked me to go with him, but I didn't. I needed to catch up with my family. Despite all, it's because of him, why I am a proud paediatric doctor today. The only time, I had ever doubted him, was when I found out about my chlamydia. I was diagnosed, after one week of us being together. However, I could have got it from any of the others.

So Jan, let's compare notes. Our journeys are so different, but we inspired each other. They got the tissues out, and wiped away each other tears, with smiles of relief on their faces.

"I'm soo, soo very sorry, you had been through all that. My life trials have been nothing like yours. I felt sheltered hearing your story. So from now on, I promise to never cry and complain, about my past ever again. Because I will always remember that, it could be worse. Onwards and upwards from now on." Jan spoke gently, while she placed her right hand, in Sandy's right hand.

Utmost Love

You were the only one, who listened to my cries for many nights,
And assured me, everything will be alright.
The one, who took me from the gutters,
Now, you caused my heart, to constantly flutter.
My darling, you were my knight,
And I love you, with all my might.

Our days were filled with love and laughter,
I still smile at the things we did,
We had such good banter…
I am forever pleased, the memories are so great,
They are indeed priceless,
I know our lives were brought into focus,
Purely through fate.
But today, and every day,
My heart rejoices, especially because of you.

CHAPTER 6

Looking to the future – a prince for Jan

A moment of contemplation for Jan, as she got out her black-leather cover diary – and made a few pointers.

Though how impatient I am, I know how imperative it is to find the right person. It's not about settling down with just anyone, being clingy, or fearful of being alone. It's not even just about sex – it really is about finding wholesome happiness, fulfillment and true companionship. Sometimes I find that, I can be too hasty... But I don't know, how long I need to be patient for. Nevertheless, should I be given another chance of love, I will most times put his needs first, and mine last. I will do this because when I love someone, I truly love. And there is nothing of myself that I couldn't forsake, if it means his happiness. I will also do this because, I don't want to lose another love – and live with the guilt that, I could have done more. I would love someone who can appreciate my qualities, and accept my flaws – like I would for him. But again, I know... I really know... I should be patient, and most of all, I should be talking to God more about this. As without His guidance, everything could go belly-up and pear-shaped.

Sometimes I feel that, there isn't a special man waiting for me. As we are all different in our ways, thoughts and lifestyle. But there are very special guys out there – I just need to find one of them. And hope that we can work together – and create beautiful memories. It's what life is about! Whenever there are hiccups, we learn to accept our differences, compromise and respect each other. Also, sensitivity is a pretty important phenomenon – so someone who will allow us to mutually consider, each other feelings carefully before acting. Especially, when the mood isn't quite right. But having said all this, I know the best happiness, is making myself happy – before attempting to make a man happy. Know my way, what I stand for – before allowing him to stand on my platform. If I don't create my own platform – then a man could stand on me, for his own platform... And this would surely, cause a lot of hurt and pain! Besides, it just won't work!!! Thus, I shall stand my grounds – and remember, time is the grand master of all things.

Jan and Sandy, brainstormed dating ideas at the park.

"I would like to get married and have some kids. People to call my own, and enjoy the rest of my life with. A lot of children, to fill the empty spaces in my house – and make it a home. I have everything most people could only dream of, but most women already have, what I'm dreaming of," Jan conversed with Sandy.

Sandy smiled emotively and suggested, they started finding ways to fill Jan's love gap. In that instance, Jan's face lit up, as she embraced hope. But first, Jan's right hand lady (Sandy) needed some vital information.

"So, who are we really looking for? Oh wait, please let me guess – man on the moon!" Sandy voiced humorously.

"I would love a guy, who is all man – if you know what I mean. He should be masculine, tall, handsome, and have the full package. Most importantly, he's got to be made up of love, loyalty, kindness and sensitivity. Someone, who will understand my needs, and certainly treat me well. A partner with similar spiritual beliefs, would be even more fantastic!" Jan replied.

Sandy, then asked about his financial status. Jan giggled and expressed that, he doesn't need to have a penny. What's hers is his, and what's his, is for both of them. And he will still never have to feel inferior, or anything – she had more than enough, to share for them as a family.

"To be quite frank, he could be a janitor… Or a cesspool truck conductor – even if he's smelly, together we'll be sweet as heavenly aromas. I would be happy for us to combine our worlds – in love and harmony. Just a soul mate, who can share everything, and make us happy. I care a lot more, about finding a loving partner than money," Jan elaborated.

Jan and Sandy, got stuck into a couple of oat snack bars – while they took a little wander around the park. But Sandy couldn't help noticing, Jan was observing every other man who walked passed. Therefore, Sandy made it obvious that she was glancing around the park, to see if there was any gardener, who fits the description of Jan's ideal man.

"No luck there!" Sandy softly shouted.

So they laughed, and made fun of it all.

"Sandy, don't you have any male, single friend – who is looking for love?" Jan cheekily asked.

"Heey, what are you thinking of? Your mind is definitely an overactive one! You are my best friend and soul-sister. I would hate if you dated any of my male friends, and it didn't turn out right. This could have a really heavy impact on our relationship, as well as their relationship with me. I very much love what we've got, and wouldn't want to risk it for anything. There's a possibility that, it's better for us to look in your own circle. Maybe even dating sites or so…" Sandy suggested.

"Okay… Okay… Think we got the message loud and clear – it was just a thought," Jan whispered humorously.

"Shall we start the search then?" Sandy asked, in an optimistic tone.

It was a bit exciting, a new challenge was on their horizon. They hi-fived each other, and giggled away for a little while. Suddenly Jan had a flashing thought, worth voicing.

"There is a singles group in Leighton, at the community Centre. It's on every Friday night 6:30 until 10:30. Would you come with me please?" Jan asked Sandy.

"I sure will. We are certainly taking this journey together," Sandy, cheerfully responded.

Two weeks later, Jan and Sandy got ready, and took on the night at a singles club. It was about an hour drive away from their homes. Upon arrival, they were asked to be registered, before entering the main room – and so they did! The ladies tried not to look too desperate, as they didn't want to attract the wrong type of men. Sandy kick-started the evening, with the first round of non-alcoholic drinks. Jan went and secured a table, next to the green-tinted windows. People glanced at them and smiled, as they slowly wandered around. Perhaps they acknowledged, Jan and Sandy were new comers. However, it wasn't long after they got settled, two ladies approached and greeted them nicely.

Several moments later, the next round of drinks was on Jan. Clouds of doubts started filling their minds, whether or not they had made the right decision. Jan and Sandy were on the brink of giving up – when suddenly they heard an unfamiliar voice, said hello. They looked side-ways, and saw a very tall, white and handsome man approached them. They eyed him from head to toe, before returning greetings. He looked at them quite pleased, and then introduced himself as Gui. He quite courteous asked, if he could kindly join their company. While Jan remained quiet, Sandy politely told him yes, he was welcome. The night had finally started! Jan asked to be excused, so she could to go and buy another round of drinks.

"Erm – My glass is nearly empty, could I get anyone a drink?" Jan politely asked.

"No, please let me..." Gui said.

Sandy, turned to Jan and spoke quietly, "Erm, I... I would like to stay, but I really can't. I have just remembered, there's something I need to do back at home, before I go to bed. So good luck Hun."

This of course, was her excuse to escape and left Jan to it. Jan told her OK, and that she will see her in the morning. They hugged gently and said their goodbyes. Sandy looked back at Jan once more, as she exited the building.

"What would you like to drink or nibble?" Gui, asked Jan.

"An orange juice, would be just right. Thank you," Jan replied graciously, as she tried to keep a lid on her nervousness.

"Alrighty – an OJ for you, Madam – and a water for me, coming right up," Gui spoke, very smoothly.

Back at the table, they talked and laughed the evening away. Gui had a very privileged upbringing, and was most times a happy person. Though, he struggled to be accepted by many people. His parents who loved him entirely, had found him a bit weird at times. They thought, there was something about him, that didn't add-up. Most of his friends, believe that he had a dark side. However, being an executive film producer gave him the perfect opportunity, to bring out that side of himself. Amongst others, he had produced a series of eight vampires and six ghost movies. Nevertheless, Gui's, favourite thing to do outside of work, was spending time with his mates. He also enjoyed going out for meals, and travelling the world. His favourite place was Australia, his country of origin – a place filled with happy childhood memories.

Gui was 42 years old and never had the chance, to remain settled in a relationship – as none of them had lasted longer than a year. He wanted to have children, but so far, it hasn't happened – except when his American ex-girlfriend Zahid, pretended she was carrying his baby for six months. She then confessed it wasn't true, and Gui had left her instantaneously. Kioni was his only ex-fiancé, and they had broken up a year ago. Gui had woken up one morning, only to noticed Kioni was gone. Her family told him, she got married to her childhood boyfriend. This had happened a month before, she moved out of Gui's home. During that time, Kioni was also six weeks pregnant for her husband. On reflection, he acknowledged, she had stopped all bedroom activities two months before her disappearance. She was the only woman Gui had ever loved entirely, and trusted with his deepest and darkest secrets. Kioni was described as attractive, medium height and slender – with beautifully short black hair, and lovely deep blue eyes. She was a property lawyer, born in a traditional White British family, and never lived outside of the United Kingdom. And so Gui believed, she was living in Central London, as she was a big fan of the city.

Jan shared much about her life's journey, so far. Included that, having a very strong and supportive father, made all the difference. She told him, some of her struggles would have been dissimilar, if her mum was alive – and life would have definitely been more satisfying. However, all things aren't so perfect, and they got to enjoy life for what it is. Gui was curious to hear more about, Jan's parents and her upbringing – likewise he was happy to be open about his… As it became apparent, both had lost at least one of their parents. Gui's father died of prostate cancer, when Gui was only eight years-old – and mother died of breast cancer, ten years later. Since then, he had been on his own – though with much support from his well-loved relatives. They were amazed by the coincidence – but it had also created a common ground, for them to talk some more.

Jan thought, he sounded ambitious and intelligent – and exhibit similar traits to herself. They had drinks after drinks, and several visits to the restroom. However, Gui asked Jan if she would like to join him, in a game of pool. She responded yes – but just one, then it was time to call it a night.

They played, and Gui had won fair and square. Nonetheless, they had some great laughter, which reflected a good night-out.

Jan smiled at him, as she gathered her things to leave. Gui enlightened her, it was one of his best nights, in a very long time. She was pleased, and in return told him thanks for a lovely evening. They stood facing each other for a minute, as if they were wondering what's next. Jan subtly hinted that, it had gone past her bed time. They shook hands, just before Gui offered to escort her home. However, Jan suggested they go home via their own transport – as her car was outside. Besides, she could also do with some quiet thought processing, whilst driving home. Gui walked Jan to her car, told her good night, and walked away. After only a few steps, he briskly walked back to Jan's, and gently knocked on the driver's window. Jan curiously opened the car door.

"Oh, you are back?" She said, in a surprised tone.

"Yes," Gui gently responded, though sounded a little hesitant.

Gui wondered, if they could exchange contact details. Jan stayed silent for a few seconds. Gui gave her a business card with his number, and suggested she gives him a ring. Jan accepted and told him, she will call him soon. He stood there hesitantly. She noticed, and decided to give him her mobile number, written down on a blank card.

Gui asked her, if they could meet again... Maybe, lunch one day soon.

"It should be alright – and maybe we could explore, the beautiful central garden water park," said Jan, whilst she looked at him somewhat flirtatiously.

"Indeed... And, then go for something to eat. A man got to eat right?" Gui said, excitedly.

Gui once again, said goodnight – this time, he got into his car and drove away. Jan drove home, and got on with her nightly routine – cleansed her face and got dressed, before going to bed. She lay on her back, stared at the high white ceiling, and wandered away, until she fell asleep.

In the morning after breakfast, Jan went next door to see Sandy. They sat down for a nice cup of coffee, tea and biscuits outside in the back garden. Sandy, had always looked after her garden beautifully. One that kept her closer to nature – as the beautiful evergreen trees, surrounded 20 acres of land. Besides, those leather garden chairs, were to die for... They sat at ease, while Jan told Sandy, all about the night before – as well as, she was looking forward to see him again. Sandy encouraged Jan to go with the flow, but she should try to understand, what her heart was feeling. Overall, there were some good and positive feelings going for Gui. The conversation was in full flow, from her jittery feelings, to dress code for their next date. Out of the blue, came a beep from Jan's phone. Gui had sent a text.

"Hi Jan, I had a great time last night. Have you thought of a date yet? Oh, I nearly forget the xxx."

Jan waited for approximately 15 minutes, before replying. He was told, to expect her call soon. And maybe, they could fix a date then. During this time, she was back at her home.

A whole week had passed, and Gui hadn't received a text message or phone call from Jan. He wondered, if she was having second thoughts – and contemplated how he might see her again. But she was in a limbo. Jan had taken time out to make sure, she was happy with what her heart was feeling. Eventually, she gave him a call. Their delightful conversation, had lasted nearly an hour. And finally, a date for the next day. Central garden water park, it was then. A place where everything magical happened – and nearly everyone, went there on a love date. Maybe it had something to do with, the love spring waterfall.

Next day, they enjoyed a beautiful bright day together. Idyllically, they were drawn to the park's natural attraction – as they wandered around. The scenery was beautiful, and everything else fell into place. It was obvious, there was some sort of connection between them. Before the day ended, it was dinner at The Mirage restaurant and bar. Over dinner, they got a little closer and flirted a lot. Quite frequently, there was some gentle touching of hands, and leaning forward towards each other. This was blissful! Plenty of happy smiles and fluidity. A happy Jan, took the opportunity and mentioned, her birthday celebration was the next upcoming event. Gui suggested, he takes her out for the day. Nonetheless, Jan had already made plans with friends and work colleagues. But there was one other thought – Jan suggested, he could be her special guest… And of course, he accepted nicely. Jan had filled him in, with all that he needed to know. Seemingly, they were up for a fulfilled weekend.

After the date, Jan was over the moon. There was a sensation, she hadn't felt in a very long time. That must be the feeling, of falling in love again. This was happening, and happening really fast. Back at home, Jan went online and filled Kyle in. They hadn't spoken for a while – and so, Kyle was thrilled, she was finally getting there. Marcello's name was mentioned in conversation, he was still single, but playing the field.

"Oh, I am going to get that – I will catch up with you again real soon. Love to the family," said Jan.

"OK. Love you. Bye… Jan wait a sec! Happy birthday for tomorrow!!! I nearly forget," Kyle replied.

Jan was in awe, she didn't think he remembered. She then quickly answered the phone to Sandy – who anticipated hearing all about the date. Sandy was pleased once again – and offered to help Jan, prepare for her birthday. Most certainly, this called for ladies' wardrobe time. They chatted the night away, and have settled on what to wear to impress, from makeup to shoes. The party will be held at a hotel, only just under an hour away. However, the day came to an end. Jan was left in peace to process her thoughts. She made a Panini and some fresh fruit juice, puts her legs up and relaxed. An hour later, she stretched and yawned, and decided to go to bed. Just before she tucked in, Gui had texted her good night. She replied, with a smiley face icon and a kiss.

Next morning – Jan's 30th birthday. She arose and had given God thanks, for allowing her to live to see another wonderful and successful year. She smiled, and embraced the beautiful autumn day, with a big burst of optimism. Certainly, she was also reminiscing about the day's event. And surely, thoughts of the very handsome Gui, were indeed prominent in her mind. Life felt good, for Jan! She went downstairs, her lavished house, and wandered around – just before the doorbell went. Jan wasn't expecting anything, but it was her birthday, so it wasn't unusual that something had arrived. At the door was the postman – he asked her to sign for a special delivery, and she did. Jan went inside and inspected the box package. There was no sender's address. Like the curious cat, Jan rapidly opened up the box – and saw a beautiful midnight blue gown, with matching jewellery. Jan unfolded the dress, she noticed there was a card, wishing her happy birthday – signed from your admirer. She looked even more anxious. Jan, immediately rang Sandy – but she was taking a bath, and so missed the call. An hour later, Jan rang again – Sandy answered, and then made her way over to Jan, in a hurry.

"Wow! This gift set is lovely," Sandy curiously commented.

She had a look at the package and its contents – and struggled to figure out, who sent them. Jan felt anxious, and put the gift behind her front door. Just before Sandy left, she asked…

"Do you think it could be Gui…? Or maybe not," she quickly mulled over her question.

Jan thought, uum… Why would he? And, they've only just met. The door shuts, as Sandy left. Jan picked up her mobile and rang Gui. First, she greeted him quite hesitantly. He wished her happy birthday – to which Jan subtly responded, it's only another day, no big deal.

"Thank you for my birthday present. It was a great surprise" – Jan spoke diplomatically. "… And my address?"

"You are most welcome. Um – your address? A letter had fallen out of your car, at the park. I saw it after you drove away," Gui explained.

Not feeling a great sense of amusement, Jan went quiet. Gui asked to be forgiven, for making a fool of himself. He explained that, it was an act of thoughtfulness and impulsiveness together – and he got carried away. Gui also managed to let her know, he really liked her.

"Ooh, sorry. Erm, you haven't made a fool of yourself. It was a surprise, that's all. But then – I supposed it was meant to be a surprise. Right? Quite an independent one – me… I wasn't expecting gifts so soon. And just for the record, as if you couldn't tell, I like you too," Jan voiced, and tittered politely.

"So, you like me, aah?" Gui said, somewhat pleasingly.

Jan paused, before telling him the gifts were lovely. Therefore, she will wear them to the party. Nevertheless, Jan was feeling slightly weary, and wanted to end the conversation. So she finally, ever so kindly suggested that, they could talk again later.

A little later, Jan indubitably enlightened Sandy – Gui, had indeed sent the gifts. Sandy's voice tone and reaction, made Jan felt a great depth of uncertainty, deep down in the pit of her stomach. Still, Jan didn't act on it. Over the next few hours, Jan watched a romcom and responded to her birthday messages. And of course, engaged in an hour long conversation with her favourite man, Jim – as she filled him in, on her latest life's events. He was glad, Jan was finding love again. Jim encouraged her, to take care of her heart – and he was looking forward to meeting Gui, at the party.

In the likeness of a fallen autumn leaves, floating with the wind – Jan danced and glide about her house, humming the words of Jim's favourite song (*you're my reason for living…*). She meticulously laid out her outfit and accessories, on the bed. Next, Jan spent the best part of one hour, getting ready. Jan's pin-up hairstyle was flawless, and her outfit, sparkling, white diamond necklace, matching black bag and shoes, completed her perfect looked. Felt glamorous, Jan stood in front of her big mirror, and twirled for the one-hundredth time. And despite the flood of anxiety, she remained composed. Jan then walked timely down the stairs – when the sound of Gui's car, she heard. He drove through the opened gates, and parked his car. Gui gave her a constant gaze, and whispered to himself…

"Just when I thought, she couldn't look any more beautiful, than she already is…"

Gui greeted Jan with a gentle hug, and a kisses on her cheeks. He wasted no time, overwhelming her with charming compliments. Jan in return complimented Gui, on how suave he looked. Even though, she couldn't help feeling that Gui was making a statement, when he wore matching colours with her (black evening jacket suit, midnight blue shirt, and matching slim tie).

However, Jan had invited Gui inside – and offered a drink. He accepted some water, as they cheered and drank a little. Gui, anticipated seeing the house entirely – and so, it was for his pleasure, he wandered around. Once the tour was over, they made their way out. Gui quickly stepped in front of Jan, and did the honours of opening the passenger front door, for her. They got going… And for a moment, Gui flattered Jan – in suggesting, her home was as beautiful, as she was. On that note, Jan conversed about Gui's expensive Mercedes. He therefore made it no secret, it was his pride and joy. And although, their conversation varied from one thing to another – there was one thing, Gui needed to get straight.

"So are we, like friends or a couple? What should I call us?" Gui asked…

Jan smiled and paused for a thought – she then asked, "What would like us to be?"

"My queen," Gui pleasantly replied.

"OK. I would like that too," Jan responded.

Upon their arrival at the hotel, Gui opened the car door for Jan once more – and escorted her inside. The DJ, was happy to get the party started, since Jan had arrived. But many eyes were on Gui, as most people curiously wondered, who this male stunner was. Suddenly, the microphone sounded – and there was an announcement. *Dinner will be served in 30 minutes.* Throughout this time, Jan caught-up with some friends, and thus had a chance to finally introduce Gui. In due course, Jan sat at the main table – to her right Jim, left Sandy, and opposite her was Gui. They all charged their glasses, and cheered Jan.

After dinner Sandy and Jim, had a chance to have a friendly one-to-one with Gui. He remembered Sandy from the dating club. Jim shook his hand – and as a welcome gesture, he topped-up Gui's glass with some cocktail. Gui initiated a conversation, about the preparation that went into Jan's party. And as a man with an eye for details, he was particularly impressed with the spacious room, and the tables that were nicely laid out – covered with white cloths, and prettily decorated with fresh flowers. He even thought, the mini baskets with sweets at the end of each table, brought forth completion. However, they drank and chatted for a while, even cracked the odd jokes in between. But Jim wasn't satisfied until he got Gui to promise, he will take care of Jan. Gui, in turn gave assurance, Jan was in safe hands.

At about 1am, the party was over – just after Jan stood up, and gave a small speech. She thanked everyone, for one of the most amazing nights. As Jan puts the microphone down – Jim went over to Jan, and gave her a tightly squeezed hug. He then whispered in her ear...

"I love you darling, and you were glowing tonight. If you continue to look and feel, like the way you are tonight – I will be happy that you are contented."

Everyone was on their way home, but Sandy stayed and helped to pack, Jan's multitude of presents in the Gui's car.

"Thank you so much Hunny, I don't know what I would have done without you. I owe you so much. I love you," Jan said to Sandy, as they hugged each other ever so tightly.

"You owe me nothing, you're my sister and I love you too. Good night, and see you tomorrow," said Sandy.

Much later in the night, Jan and Gui, continued to talk about the party. But it was getting quite late.

"Would you like to stay the night?" Jan asked...

"Yes, please. Why not?" Gui instantly responded.

"Great! It would give me a chance to say, thank you properly," Jan spoke, whilst looking at Gui, flirtatiously.

They sat down and got comfortable, while the TV played in the background. Time slowly went by, their two cups of teas on the coffee table got cold. There was better entertainment, as they snuggled up on the sofa, and was mesmerised by each other. At nearly 4am, Jan showed Gui to his room, and gave him some pajamas for the night. It was easy for them to say good night, but difficult staying apart. The love birds turned away, and walked in opposite directions towards their bedrooms. Before they suddenly looked back at each other, fascinatingly. They swiftly walked back, folded into each other arms and kissed passionately.

"Can my arms have the pleasure, of holding you tight a bit longer please?" Gui asked.

A nervous Jan, dodged the question – and instead, commented on Gui's beautiful light brown eyes. She slowly let go of his hands, and went to her room. Gui was left standing alone for a minute, before he went to his own bed.

Next morning they awoke about 9am. Jan took a shower from her ensuite bathroom, dressed and went downstairs. She prepared toasts, smoked salmon strips and lemon cream – alongside a medium bowl of fruit salad, and freshly made orange juice. Jan laid them out meticulously on the table – just before she went upstairs, and knocked on Gui's opened room door. She went in – Gui held her hands and gently pulled her, onto the bed. They tumbled and snuggled, for a moment. Shortly after, Gui took a quick shower, before he got dressed and joined Jan for breakfast. Sat directly opposite each other, Gui complimented her glowing morning look, and the lovely breakfast. It was almost as if, they had known each other a long time. Together, their sense of humour was amazing – as they did silly jokes and laughed their heads off. Once breakfast was over, they brought in all the presents from his car. Gui noted, it was nearly midday. He hinted, outstaying his welcome wasn't an option. But just before he went, they showed off their lovingness, and engaged in another round of snug. Somehow, they complemented each other – and brought forth a different kind of radiance, Jan hadn't experienced.

A mystical moment arrived,
With lots of glittering hope,
And, fulfilment promised,
A moment in time – love was revived.

My heart is suffused with glee,
And profound, love is my only plea,
So for you, my darling,
Your entrance here is free.
Now that you are here to stay,
Please, keep my heart beating in a gentle rhythm,
And abundance love, is sure for you each day.
… With us standing tall – and feeling strong,
Be sure to know, my heart is the place where you belong.

CHAPTER 7

A good life: Light shade emotions

Jan and Gui's hearts, were in constant flutter – these days, reflected a high-point of their relationship. Together, they spent more time travelling the world, than the president did across the United States. They were unstoppable, as money was never an issue! It was spent uncontrollably, whilst they filled their lives with unlimited romantic gestures. And blissfully gave each other, nothing but the best of everything they desired. Love was shining like the sun, in their hearts – and the temperature was either just right or sexy hot. It was their sole aim to fully embrace this new life, new love, wrapped up in new hope, for an incredible new future. Well, at least, it seemed that way. From time to time, Jan had stopped and pinched herself – her heart was once more possessed with love. Happiness waved over their lives – and filled them up with an exhilarating sensation, like that of which surfers get, when riding the waves in Australia oceans.

Gui was the perfect prince on many levels – with his sharp wit and fabulous sense of humour, laughter was never ceased. Seemingly possessed with thoughtfulness, in abundance – Jan was always first and foremost, in Gui's mind. Some mornings, Jan woke up to the smell of beautiful fresh roses, or an elaborate bouquet of pink and yellow tiger lilies. Other times, there may be a romantic note, left on her bedside table – should he had gone to work, before Jan was awake. But nothing said it all for Gui, like giving Jan breakfast in bed, surprise lunch dates, and his funny naked chef evening meals. Those days were often unscheduled, so Jan would not be able to make any prediction. He was a brilliant cook, with exquisite taste in food – and was especially good with main meals. Gui never hesitated to ensure, his desserts left a lasting effect on Jan's taste buds. However, he very meticulous, and could be seen as a perfectionist. Timing was everything. But there was no question, as to how much Gui had enjoyed seeing his queen, relished and appreciated everything he did for her. It made it all worthwhile!

This wonderful new life-treatment was reciprocal. Jan had her ways of making Gui felt like, the only one in her world. His life was her priority – she absolutely adored him. Jan's sensuality and spontaneous ability to act, meant Gui was never once left short of a surprise. Quite frequently, he was left feeling overwhelmed, of course, in the sweetest of ways. Jan made certain her presence was always felt. Infinite love was paramount, as she flooded him with attention, somewhat in very tactile ways. On a regular basis, Jan had given Gui a full body massage, facial, manicure and pedicure – all from the comfort of her own hands. And of course, surprised treats such as candle-lit dinners, and grand cruise get away, were certain. However, Jan also liked doing simpler favours – every Sunday, she hand washed Gui's car, and filled it up with petrol. Added to the list, there were endless emails and text messages, that weren't just romantic and sensational – but reminders of how well-loved and appreciated, Gui was. Jan completed Gui's life and left little room, for dissatisfaction. In her mind, it was the meaning behind these gestures that really mattered. For all this, Gui was indeed contented!

Jan enjoyed flaunting her body for Gui – and where sex was concerned, life was filled with excitement. Dressing up and getting into characters, was a part of the fun. She could be a nurse, doctor, housemaid, paramedic assistant or just his sexy masseuse. Her imaginary fantasies were beyond limits. On some occasions, whilst been out on dates, Jan would only be partially dressed – all on, except her knickers. This was usually found, in one of Gui's pockets. He would occasionally offer, to put them on her. As the unstoppable lovers engaged in saucy conversation, they often flirted their way to Venus and Mars. Their signal that the bedroom was calling them (*phrase use to go home and have sex*), was generally initiated with under the table leg works.

They made hell seemed like an arctic place. Everywhere in their home was entirely explored – where sexual activity was concerned. From the kitchen floor, work-tops, living and dining room, to their private back garden at nights. At the centre of their activities, were whipped cream, chocolate sauce and honey – and these were used, in no uncertain term. One Saturday afternoon, they had forgotten Gui's childhood friend Tony, was coming over for a visit. Gui and Jan, had gotten heated on the living room carpet. He was wearing nothing, but smooth dark chocolate from face to toes. While Jan was covered, with a thick layer of whipped cream, from her neck to waistline. And surely, she wasn't without a pair of black six-inch heels and fishnet tights. Besides, they were Gui's number one, on his hot list. About 15 minutes into their fun-time, Tony had entered the house, before shouted anyone home. Shattered by his appearance, embarrassment shaded their faces.

Tony swiftly turned his head away and apologised – before justifying his entrance. Seemingly, Jan and Gui had left the gate and front door opened. Tony appeared a little sheepish, but was pleased to see Jan, in all her glory. Gui was fuming with anger – he looked at Tony reprehensibly, whilst he hurried to the kitchen and tied on Jan's mini, pink-floral-apron, around his waist. Jan, couldn't feel anymore discomfited – she speedily grabbed a pair of red cushions off the sofa, and covered most of her modesty. She hurried to the upstairs bathroom, and took a long shower. Tony told them, he will wait in the lounge – while he helped himself to a can of coke, before lazed out on the sofa. After about thirty minutes, Jan and Gui, had composed themselves and caught up with Tony, as planned. It turned out to be a very interested day. But what Tony saw, was definitely not up for discussion.

Nearly two years on, Jan and Gui were still living in separate homes. In conversations, they jokingly expressed their thoughts about living together. In spite of this, it seemed neither of them wanted to make the first move. One day Jim went by, and had noticed how happy and comfortable, they were with each other. He had asked, why aren't they doing it properly, and lived in the same home. They both looked at Jim, as to say – we've been thinking of this idea too. They felt pleased, Jim was on board. However, Jan spoke openly that she wasn't sure, whether Gui would want to move away, from his posh penthouse. Stood at the breakfast bar in the kitchen, chopping carrots –Gui gentle cuddled Jan from behind and whispered...

"If this is my invitation to move in with you darling, yes... Yes, is the answer."

Later that day, after Jim went back to his home, Gui and Jan had some time to talk properly, about moving him in. They had decided, this will happen in two weeks. In the meantime, Gui had another thing on his mind. Gui told Jan he was going out, but should be back home in an hour or so. He then went to see Jim, and asked for Jan's hand in marriage. Gui told Jim, he would like for them to be married, before moving in... No hesitation, just an instant yes, was Jim's answer. Two days later, whilst Jan was at work, Gui went to see Sandy. He told her of his plan, to ask Jan to marry him. She was over the moon about his idea. An hour later, Sandy, Gui and his best friend Zack met in the city, to buy Jan's engagement ring – as previously discussed. After an hour of eye shopping, they finally found the most stunning diamond ring. White gold, boasting ruby-emerald heart shape gems in the centre. The ruby was a slightly smaller heart, placed in the middle of the emerald, as two hearts joined together. Surrounded with beautiful bold-transparent diamonds. It was by far, the most exceptional and expensive ring. They were stunned by the ring they had found, but all approved.

It was now official, a big day was coming soon. First, an engagement party was considered – and they were going large. Gui, Zack and Sandy, in very little time, had the engagement party plans perfectly covered – as they had booked a private villa in Paris, for the weekend. Except for Her Majesty Jan, all of their closest friends and family were invited. Once all was confirmed, Gui told Jan, he was taking her away for a few days. Alongside that, Jan should treat herself to whatever she desired – and it was all on him. Gui wanted to make sure, nothing was left undone. So, he ran Jan a warm bath, with scented lavender oil and red rose petals. All this, wasn't without its final touch – some warm towels, and aromatic candle lights. And surely, there was room for one more – he poured her a tall glass of chilled champagne. Once Gui was satisfied, he had finally left Jan to relax. A short while later, Jan was out of her bath – and they had some well-deserved intimate time. However, Gui didn't call it a night, until he packed their suitcases with all the necessities – while Jan remained clueless.

Next morning, the blissful couple were up and ready to go. But Gui wasn't just going to forget, his tummy was rumbling. And so he hinted subtly, that he could eat... Jan suggested, she will treat them to breakfast at the airport – whilst in business lounge. No time wasted, as a cab arrived outside their gate. At the airport, they enjoyed a light sandwich breakfast, just before their flight. And few hours later, they were in Paris. Outside the airport arrivals, there was a man holding a white square card, with their names written on it – a private taxi awaited. Gui spotted their chauffeur, and they made their way over. The chauffeur opened the door for Jan, and was rather polite. In conversation, he asked about their reason for being in Paris – Jan flirted with him funnily, and replied, her visit was to meet someone like himself. However, after a short drive, they arrived at the villa. They were very satisfied, with its opulent style. Simply, the kind of place Jan loved – beautiful, with spectacular views!

Outside of the premises, were six private swimming pools, and high edges for optimum privacy. Inside the villa, was lush and spacious – their bedrooms and bathrooms, reflected class at its highest standard. Gui had requested their bed and floor, to be sprinkled with red rose petals. Also added, were the little things that mattered – Mr and Mrs bathrobes and slippers. Once they had seen it all, there were lots of hugs and kisses – which lead to passionate love-making. Much later, Jan was enjoying a moment on the sofa, when she had a thought about dinner. A nearby restaurant, came to her thought... But suddenly there were sounds, like people walking on the balcony. Curious Jan, went and had a look – surprisingly, it was the villa's staff. They had decorated the balcony with flowers and lights, and a table for two. Dinner was served – lobster meals and white wine. The mood was set, with the sound of soft soul music, played in the background. Jan began to feel a bit suspicious, though she smiled without saying it out aloud. Gui was walking slowly behind Jan – then suddenly, he stepped slightly in front, held her around the waist, and kissed her lips gently.

"Darling, I was just about to tell you that, erm, dinner will be served here tonight. I hope that's OK?" Gui said, in a quiet sounding voice.

Absorbing it all – Jan was indeed delighted, and continued to give Gui her undivided attention. During dinner, Jan and Gui took pleasure in feeding each other, made silly jokes, and filled the evening with warmth. Hence, the weekend was off to a great start – and Gui, was undeniably satisfied.

Saturday morning – day of the engagement. Room service at the ready, as their breakfast was served in bed. Nothing was more indulging, than a big breakfast platter of croissants, buttered-jammed bread rolls, tomato, egg sandwich, fruit salad, orange juice and latte. And though, they could sit there all day, and be pampered some more – but Gui wanted them away out. Shortly after breakfast, they went and did a few things – included shopping. Gui, had bought Jan a white gold jewellery set. Jan got Gui, some top of the range ties and cufflinks – alongside, his favourite fragrances. Then continued to stroll around – soon, Jan stopped by a men's store, to shop even more. But Gui hesitantly told her, they had done enough shopping for one day. She curiously took his words, and continued to eye shop from outside.

Unlimited time wasn't on their side... Nevertheless, as they wandered around, their eyes became fixated on some vintage Citroën – managed by a lovely male Parisian, who noticed they were staring at the cars. He asked them to come for a drive. They chose an open top, vintage convertible Citroën. The Parisian chauffeured them around, to some of Paris most romantic spots, included the famous water hole. Not one moment wasted, on things that didn't concern them. They soaked up the culture, and filled their morning with lots of romantic gestures and affection. It was an awesome atmosphere! A dreamlike day, they didn't want to end. Nonetheless, the clock was ticking – and an anxious Gui, hated being late. He knew they needed to be back at the villa, by lunchtime – just after their guests arrived.

Back at the villa, Gui and Jan approached the main door. Jan thought, she had spotted someone familiar, walking on the side balcony. But then she thought, maybe it was deja vu. In the main lounge that was facing the front door – everyone was waiting quietly. Just as Jan attempted to open the door, Jim opened it instead – and everyone shouted surprise. The happy engagement banners, said it all. Jan stood in awe for a short moment, and looked around at everyone in the room, before she uttered…

"Oh my goodness me! Really? I should have known, something was up!"

Gui instantly went down on one knee, got out the most gorgeous ring from his pocket – and asked her to marry him. She smiled and nervously accepted. Everyone cheered and toasted them – and the party got started. A little later, Jan and Gui chatted about his plans – and how he pulled it off. But once again, Gui was ready to drop another sky-high surprise.

"I have organised everything, because I don't see why we should wait to enjoy life later, when we can start enjoying it all now. Life is short, and I just want to spend the rest of mine, with you darling. Before I say what the surprise is, if your answer is no – it will be OK with me. And I will wait, for your decision. So please, say as you truly feel. Eem, I - I had arranged for a marriage minister to come and wed us, tomorrow afternoon. Should you say no, I can call and cancel straight away, or even first thing tomorrow. It's not a problem, as long as you are happy."

Could Jan withstand any more huge surprises, in one day? She wasn't quite sure what to say. Jan asked for a moment, to think about it. Much later, prior to everyone departing to their private quarter, Jan gathered all the guests for her speech. Followed by her big unexpected announcement.

"Thank you all, from the bottom of our hearts for making this day – what is… Now, you all had a great surprise for me – but thanks to my gorgeous fiancé, it's now your turn to be surprised. I hope your tickets will allow you, to stay until Monday morning at least. Our wedding will be tomorrow afternoon, at 2pm. Venue, the Marande Deluxe six star hotel, just next door the villa. We would like to thank you, for your kind support. It means so much, to see the effort you put into our engagement celebration. To my dad, I love you! Please, let's raise our glasses to our absent loved ones! Love you guys, and good night."

There was a surprise! Gui had no idea, Jan would say yes in an announcement. He thought, she would have told him first. Everyone filled up their glasses, and once again, toasted the happy couple. Gui stood next to his fiancé, he held her hands and expressed his infinite love. His speech was quite warm and heartfelt – as they kissed each other, rather passionately. Gui also thanked everybody, especially his father-in-law to be. A little while later, Gui, Jan and Jim had a moment to talk about things, so far. Jan was amazed and grateful for the opportunity, to create a mental image of the build-up to the day. However, she was the least of Jim's concerns for the night – as he contemplated his *father of the bride* speech, and looked forward to walking Jan down the aisle. The party was over – and before Jan had some real alone time with her fiancé, she walked Jim to his room.

Sunday morning – and there was a knocking at the door. Their breakfast was served – two trays, nicely arranged with some of their favourite things. Approximately twenty minutes later, there was a second knocking at the door. Jan hesitated not, as she straight away went and answered. It was a delivery – a beautiful floral bouquet, and a small gift basket nicely packed, with all her favourite goodies, and champagne. A little white folded card, was attached – it stated:

"Darling, if you have received this gift of love, it meant that Saturday night was a success! My Love, thanks for being my light, in a very dark world. Do I have to say, I LOVE YOU? I think you already know by now, just how much I do xxx Gui."

Approximately 25 minutes later, there was a third knocking... Gui, asked Jan to get the door – and so she did! It was the third and final delivery – Jan's wedding gown, shoes and accessories. The stunning, mostly laced, half-white gown, carefully designed with a long train, was seemingly very attractive. It was like a centrepiece! Jan was astounded that he managed to be so spot on, with the things she desired. He was definitely a partner, who paid attention keenly.

Before Jan could get fitted in her dress, there was just enough time for a swim. If they had never felt the wonderful unfathomable feeling of love, they did then – on the most glorious autumn day. A few hours later, Sandy and Zack were at the ready to help beautify Jan and Gui. Zack did a great job, keeping Gui in check – while he maintained his very suave look – in his grey jacket suit, matching shoes, light-orange tie and half-white shirt.

In time, everyone had made their way to the hotel – where they were offered drinks and was directed to the wedding hall. Once the wedding was in progress – Jan and Gui, slowly walked in from two different entrances.

They made it to the podium, at the same time – with their maid of honour and groomsman, right behind them. After their vows, Gui was very pleased he finally puts on £20,000 wedding band, on Jan's finger. Gui wasn't keen on wearing rings, and so decided against a wedding band for himself. Jan's rings were eye stunners – something, one and all talked about. But there were just as much to say, in the light and friendly receptive speeches. Jim spoke pleasingly, and wished his beloved daughter and new husband a great life.

Monday morning – family and friends were on their way home. Gui and Jan, stayed in Paris for another three days. Then Venice for a week, and New York for four days – before returning to their country home. The newlywed took time out to unwrapped presents, and sent out thank you cards. And although, neither of them was to be at work until Tuesday morning – they had popped into Gui's workplace. All his work colleagues, were taken by surprise – and even more so, hearing of their marriage. His boss and mates, happily hid behind their questionable thoughts, and fore-fronted politeness. Congratulations were in order – and as goodwill gesture, a lunch was done in their honour. Mack, Gui's oldest work colleagues, had shown special interest in Jan. Gui tried to make a joke, and hinted Mack wanted to take his wife away... They all laughed – even though, Jan had hidden well, she was a little embarrassed. Nevertheless, all eyes were on Jan and Gui, as their body language spoken volume. They were unable to keep their eyes off each other – it just seemed like untainted love. Most people admired them, as the perfect couple.

Gui and Jan, were very down to earth. Especially Jan, who was actually quite personable – and saw the best in people. Gui was ultra-sensitive and didn't seem the type, who would hurt anyone. However, there was something unpredictable hidden, behind his charming smile and corporate look. Well, there were no complaints from Jan about her new husband, so maybe there was nothing to worry about. What had worked perfectly, was Jan's attitude to disagreement. She generally agreed with Gui, regardless of the matter. Whenever there were verbal conflicts, she would walk away. But moments later, they apply the old communication method – to solving their problem. There was a set of rules, which they lived by. Never go to bed, while feeling angry with each other. Never leave the house without sharing a cuddle, say I love you and goodbye. And finally, never raise their voices at each other, and say words that aren't really meaningful – and particularly hurtful. And like good communication, forgiveness was very important.

However, there was a tiny matter of name change or not. Jan had decided to keep her surname, in honour of Jim – she was his only close family. Gui was a bit taken aback by this idea. Although, he didn't make it an issue. He had always thought, his wife would take his name, Momoid – in case of them having children, they would all have the same family name. Nonetheless, Jan hadn't completely dismissed the idea – she just hope to hold on to it for a bit longer. And if children were involved, then she will revert to the name change notion. Jan would like to have two children, a girl and a boy – and hoped to take them swimming and gymnastics. Gui would like four boys – he dreams of teaching them how to surf, and probably get them into playing basketball.

The years rolled on – and there was no sign of a baby. To some extent, it was the epitome of their frustration. Considered they had an active sex life, without the use of contraception. For over two years, it was the topic of most conversations. So they had brought the issue, to their doctor's attention. All plausible options were laid out, on the doctor's table for analysis. Included fertility clinic, adoption and fostering – these choices brought a glint of hopelessness, to Gui's mind. They looked at each other, as if to say – this might be a long and stressful journey, for us. Hand in hand comforted each other, they decided to keep trying for another few months. Gui suggested, they continued with a healthy sex life, exercise regularly, and adopt good-effective relaxation techniques. Jan sighed, with a great depth of heaviness. Frustration was on the rise – and was more so, for Jan. As she acknowledged, her inability to make Gui's dream come true. After some very deep thinking, she came to the realisation that, their lives weren't perfect after all. And despite their wealth – she might never get the chance to experience, what other biological mums have felt and enjoyed.

One day Sandy reminded Jan, how wonderful and special she was.

"Having children is a wonderful thing, but should it not happen now, didn't mean you are any less of a woman. God has a plan for everyone. These plans are all different, in some ways. Take time to understand, what God wants from you – and for you. Quite often our plans and desires are different, from that of our Master's. Everything won't unfold in a day, a month or even a year. Whilst there's life, there's hope."

Jan thanked Sandy, for being supportive throughout – before she expressed her thoughts.

"It can sometimes take years to build faith, hope and trust. Yet, we can lose them in just one instant, and that's what I'm terrified will happen to Gui and I. If..." Jan paused and sighed, as she held back on finishing her sentence.

As a Christian, and was more so committed after their marriage – Jan relied heavily on her faith. The way had always been through prayer, hard work and determination. Often times, she comforted herself with this thought – in the midst of countless fallen moments, there were many victorious times. Gui wasn't as strong-spirited, as Jan. Nevertheless, he remembered valuable lessons, which was taught to him by his Christian parents. The importance of worshipping God, in spirit and in truth, not that he had always lived accordingly. Still together, they had found a renewed strength – which had given them, even more courage to live for God. Morning and nightly worship were no longer, Jan on her own. A routine was in place – Morning Prayer, before they got out of bed, and evening bible session just before bedtime.

Being a huge part of their church, they played a few active and vital roles. Gui was the leading choir director, a job he executed brilliantly. He was possessed with great leadership qualities, and everyone loved him. Together they worked as a team, for praise and worship session on Sunday mornings. It was lively – and everyone sung, danced and praised God. They even got a chance to greet each other. Some people hadn't said hello to another, all week – up until then. It was good to put a smile, on some lonely faces. Their job didn't stop there! They were huge contributors, to the church charity – financially and literally. The charity catered for lonely, ill and desperate people. Jan and Gui, had given hands-on care to those who required it, and dedicated time to love, listened and laughed. They shared much affection, with those they cared for – and were humbled by the lives.

Thank you for investing your time in me,
Or else, my mind would be blinded to the things, I ought to see.
You are my most infinite, and wonderful God,
And without you, standing right by my side,
My troubles, would be like invisible mountains,
No other can see.
Lord, I thank you,
For allowing me, to lay them down at your throne,
That you may take them all,
And make them your own.
As I rise with the sun, I'm privileged to see – the love you have given me,
So thank you God, for raining down your blessings on me.

CHAPTER 8

Brink of emotional destruction: Motor Neuron Disease

After three years living together, Jan and Gui, were no further forward with having a child. This had caused a huge strain, on their relationship. Gui insisted, he wasn't interested in any other option. Jan was open to other possibilities, particularly adoption. Especially, if it would be the case, where they were involved in the pregnancy, from conception onward. Being super keen, to do whatever it takes to give Gui have a family, Jan had taken up yoga relaxation. She was eating healthily, and playing by the books. They did everything, to prepare them for pregnancy. Still, it just didn't happen. Jan questioned whether there was a biological fault, with either or both of them. She once suggested to Gui, they ought get tested – should there be a problem with their reproductive system. A nervous Gui, hesitated and disagreed. Unspoken thoughts, unkind non-verbal gestures, and suspicious behaviour had spoken volume. Gui presumed, there was a problem with Jan reproduction. Jan took it quite seriously and decided, not to pressure Gui into thinking about the adoption. She then secretly, had a thorough medical examination done. Jan's results showed, her chances of getting pregnant were high.

Jan started experiencing, a new Gui. He began to be very withdrawn, obnoxious and verbally abusive. Gui would speak to Jan angrily, and used very sharp words – for deep-wound effect. At times she felt threatened, only that she hoped he wouldn't physically hurt her. Sexual activities, meals together, going to church had literally become non-existent. A smile for each other, fun and laughter, were all things of the past. They occasionally shared the same bedroom, yet not the same cover. Some weeks, Gui would be away without any correspondence – and show little or no regards to their relationship. In spite of this, Jan didn't want to give up – and decided to try harder to have him back... She did everything to entice Gui, but he had completely ignored her. His life had been about work, friends and having plenty of rest. Days passed, and there was no conversation between them. Jan was slowly but surely, slipping away in the background of their lives. Invisible to her husband, she felt isolated, despondent, frustrated and utterly embarrassed.

Emotions were soaring high, until it became unbearable – Jan didn't have the courage, to share this particular problem straight away, with Jim and Sandy. The last thing she wanted, was to pull them into her world of misery. And she didn't want to be judged – as their marriage was supposed to reflect total happiness. One Saturday night, Jan went to bed. However, she was unable to sleep, and so spent hours praying and crying on her own. The pillows were like a punctured waterbed – soaked with tears. A distressed Jan, tried to convince Gui to come home, but there was no success. Instead, he told her to tuck herself into bed nicely, as he won't be back home until Monday evening – about tea time. Jan was persistent – she texted again, and asked him kindly to sit down and talk with her... And let her know, what it was that she could do, to make their relationship work again. Gui texted and asked Jan, to show him a positive pregnancy test. He would like a wife, who can give him kids. She broke down in tears, once more. Tempted to tell him, it wasn't her fault – but she didn't... Out of fear that, he might get very angry...

Jan recognised that their problem, was indeed her ultimate battle. Waves of weariness soaked through her muscles – her body lacked strength, and her mind became opaque. Jan's heart sunk deeper and deeper into despair, even by the slightest thought of Gui. She fleetingly stared at his large portrait, hung on the wall faced their bed – and suddenly felt suffocated, by a great rush of anxiety. Jan, swiftly grabbed her mobile phone and rang Sandy. Though it was late – after 11pm. Sandy answered, and heard a grimed sound in Jan's voice. She instantly felt worried, and invited her over to stay the night. A pot of tea and crackers awaited. Soon after, a light-handed knock at the door sounded – Sandy greeted Jan curiously, though with open arms.

Tears gushed down her cheeks, as the look of distressed masked her face. Sandy, sat Jan down on the sofa and comforted her in silence.

Eventually, Jan declared herself broken-hearted – she uninspired Sandy, with the entire story. Sandy breathes a huge sigh of displeasure, as she watched Jan mourned over her shattered dream – the dream of a strong and lasting partnership. Sandy gently wiped away Jan's tears, and warmed her heart with some encouraging words.

"Loneliness isn't necessary, if it can be avoided. Particularly, in the time of distress. So there is no need to suffer in silence. And there is no better time, to use the friendship card to your advantage, like when you feel everything that was solid beneath your feet, had turned into sinking sand."

Sandy shared her bed with Jan, and they talked the night away, before falling asleep.

Next morning, Jan awoke quite early before Sandy, and went home. A spontaneous moment arrived, she was going away on a short break. Jan rang Jim and ordered him to pack – she was on her way to pick him up. They drove to the Lake District – where peace, tranquility and stunning countryside views, were certain. They stayed at a local hotel, which was quiet and homely. The perfect time and place, for Jan to break the news to Jim. He was flustered, by Jan's unhappiness. Felt disappointed and saddened, Jim did not say much. He puts his cheek next to Jan's cheek, and held her while she cried intensely. Finally, a few words from Jim – he encouraged Jan to relax and enjoy the break.

Therefore, they planned to make their time memorable. First day, they visited Beatrice Potter's Museum – a childhood dream, for Jan. On the second day, a long walk to the lakes, had cleared their minds. And on the final day, they relaxed in a nearby café – and soaked up the friendly atmosphere. It had only taken a moment, before Jim charmed the ladies – and whoooo them all, with stand-up comedy. Something he hadn't done, since Janis died. He was so good, everyone gathered round and gave some big cheers – even Jan had perked up. Jan looked at him and smiled – the first proper beam, since they had been on their break. However, she glanced at her watch and juddered, as it was time they signed out of the hotel, before being charged for overstaying. They prepared themselves, for the journey ahead.

Jim had a window, to reminisce and laugh about the good old days, as a comedian (his second profession). However, the fun vibes only lasted a short while. Because once again, Jan slumped in defeat – and her face suddenly dropped, like wilted flowers needed water. She contemplated, Gui's days of silence. He had not called once, since they were away. Jan sat in the driver's seat, with her quivery hands holding on to the steering wheel. Jan quickly regained control, and started the car engine. But Jim felt worried, and ever so softy offered to drive... Jan quietly replied, no. And so they got going... Five hours later, they arrived at Jim's home. They hugged with such heaviness – as Jim wished her a safe journey... Jan waited until he entered his house, before she drove away.

Jan arrived home – the gate and front door were wide opened. She wondered, why that was. Gui wasn't in the mood to give explanations – but he was definitely up for a protest. He began shouting and called Jan barren. In the heat of the moment, he pushed past her in a hurry, and she fell on the sofa. Gui looked at her shockingly, and felt sorry. Suddenly there was a soft gazed – he gently stroked her face with his fingers, and apologised unaffectedly. Jan ran up the grand-sweeping stairs, laid herself down on the rugged cream carpet, and streamed away. In an attempt to ease himself of guilt – Gui spoke to Jan in a dull voice, and admitted he was consumed with selfishness and anger. Now, aspects of his personality were revealed, that he wasn't proud of. Jan slowly raised her head, and gave him the look of fear, hurt and disgust. A distressed Jan, got up and went to bed. A bit later, she was ready to talk. Jan expressed that, she loved him with or without children. However, taking his disrespectful and abusive ways into consideration, she was now officially uncertain of their future together.

Gui delved deep for the courage, to ask Jan for her forgiveness. As a man of pride and arrogance, he didn't find it easy. Nevertheless, he did! Jan's desperation for Gui's love and attention, was on the rise – and as of such, she gave an easy yes. Although, Jan had one request – that Gui, got rid of any secret. Gui hesitated – before declaring, there was no secret. A hesitant no, usually meant yes, in Jan's mind. But she gave him the benefit of the doubt. Much later in the evening, they seemed a little overwrought – therefore, they break the ice with a night out at the little Italian restaurant – ten minutes away, on the breakaway bridge. And whilst they made an effort to eat, most of their food remained untouched – except for desserts. They listened to the river ran deep and wide, the tranquillity gave Gui the loving urge to kiss Jan – but was unsure whether there were still sad emotions, lingering beneath the surface. Moments later, Jan stood up in preparation for them leaving – Gui folded his arms around hers, as they made their way home. At bedtime, they slept separately. Jan's, reverie of a great marriage, was far from reality. There were more fogs of uncertainty, than the rays of sunlight.

Next morning, it was work as usual. The bright morning sun, had brought forth some good vibes. Jan was first to mention, just how beautiful the day was. Gui was enjoying the lovely morning too. It was obvious that they were making an effort with each other, but even more apparent, that something was badly broken.

In the evening, Jan was first home. She had brought some chocolate doughnuts, for Sandy. However, whilst they were relaxing in Sandy's living room – a green Toyota car drove up and slowed down, at Jan's gate. They curiously went to see, who it was. But the Asian-looking, female driver didn't tarry. A puzzled Jan, went home immediately and called Gui. Jan was very descriptive, in telling Gui about this mysterious lady – and although, Gui sounded as if he knew who she was, he denied knowing her. Gui, then swiftly dismissed their conversation, and told Jan, he was really busy at work. She stood at her wide bay windows for a while, and hoped for some clarity. Three hours later to be precise, Gui was home, but he looked somewhat guarded. Once more, Jan asked, if the lady was known to him. He slowly held Jan's hands, and asked her to sit down in the living room. Gui told her, he wasn't being completely honest before. And he would like for her to listen carefully, before making any decision. At that point, Jan had already concluded the worst-case scenario, in her mind. She agreed to listen anyway.

Six months ago, Gui had met a 24-year-old lady, name Shamha. She was a primary school teacher. During the course of their conversations, Gui had discussed his and Jan's non-pregnancy situation. However, very little information was withheld from Shamha – so, she knew where they lived, worked and all else. Over the last few months, their friendship grew, as they got closer. Nonetheless, last night, he was supposed to meet with Shamha, but didn't get the chance. Gui, had texted her and explained, he was sorting things out with Jan. Shamha was far from feeling pleased, about being left in the lurch. She had messaged him several times, but Gui had ignored them – whilst left his phone on silent. Later that night, he eventually rang her back, and apologised profoundly. Gui somehow didn't feel surprised, Shamha had felt hurt and needed clarification. Hence the reason, she went to Jan's home. But didn't have the audacity, to buzz at the gate. Gui explained, he can't ignore Shamha, because she was pregnant for him. His apologies were fast and frequent, as he hoped Jan would still hold on their lives together.

An upset and furious Jan, was frozen. Her voice turned quiet, as her tears freely flowed… She gently pulled her hands away, and asked him what was next. Gui repeatedly told Jan, he loved her. Jan had a chance to ask him, if she was to be blamed for their inability to have children naturally. He hesitated, then said he wasn't sure… Jan told him of her secret check-up, and that she was in the clear. There were no obvious reasons, why she can't have children. They hung in silence. Jan felt empty, as she sluggishly walked towards the rectangular mirror, hung on the wall in the hall. She stared at herself for a while. Soon, she probed for details of the pregnancy. Gui spoke hesitantly that, Shamha was five months pregnant with a boy. And she was living on Manor road, about 20 minutes' drive from his penthouse.

Gui would like Jan, to accept the baby and remain a family. But there were questions. Was Shamha in love with Gui? Would she allow Jan, to be involved with their son? Jan told him, she needed time to take it all in. Uncertain of what do to, she decided to pray about it. Gui, respected her space until she had a clear mind – and was ready to make a decision. Jan was distraught about the entire situation, but even more upset that, Shamha was years younger than both herself and Gui.

Next morning, just before Jan went to work, she went for a run to clear her mind. Still, she felt muddled and tentative. Therefore, she resorted to Jim and Sandy for some support, hours later during her lunch break. Jim, Sandy and Jan had a three-way telephone conversation – he reminded her that, happiness is surely what matters, and if she can bring herself to be happy again, then her life was fulfilling its purpose. Sandy suggested, if Gui was a shoe, she would burn it – and scrubbed the ground so hard, that not even the dust or ash could be seen.

For about three weeks, Jan contemplated what to do. Finally, one afternoon, she had made a dinner reservation for 6pm – and asked Gui to meet her there. At the restaurant, they had ordered some cold drinks to start, then talked about their day at work. Awhile later, the conversation had turned to Gui's new life. And so, Jan got straight to the point – and asked Gui to allow her and Shamha to meet. There and then, Gui rang her, and explained the situation briefly. He then asked Shamha, to meet with them the next evening for dinner, at Jan's home. At first, she was slightly diffident about the invitation – nevertheless, she agreed. They got back to eating their dinner, and enjoyed all three courses. Just before leaving, Gui tried to kiss Jan, but she wasn't having it.

A moment later, they drove home, but Jan seemed quiet and tensed for most of the evening. Before bedtime, she read her Bible and prayed – while Gui had stayed up a bit later, once again. But eventually went to bed earlier, than the night before. Later in the night, Jan woke up and went to use the toilet. But then noticed, there were some unusual medication, left in the bathroom next to the face basin. They were Gui's – he was getting treated for syphilis, gonorrhoea and Chlamydia. Jan was mortified! And though unsettled, she went back to bed.

After another disconcerted night, Jan thought, oh no this was just going on and on. There was no end to Gui's surprises. Jan made breakfast for two, with all their favourite things, and nicely laid them out on the dining table. She thought, well, should this be our last meal together, they might as well enjoy it. Gui went down, and they enjoyed breakfast – it was a great start to the day. Jan then asked him about his medications. Gui spoke out loudly in fury, and told her sorry – he wasn't the man, she thought he was. Another apology, once again. Jan told him, she needed him to be clearer in his explanation. Gui confessed, he had a drunken one-night stand with a female friend, but once he sobered up, he noticed she was dressed up as a man – but it would never happen again. It was a moment of madness, he wasn't gay, and that he would like to still be with her. In response, Jan ordered him to pack his things, and leave her home instantly. Jan added, he was either straight or gay – and either way, she didn't want to know any more about him. So he was to kindly, keep his messy and unfaithful life away from her home, friends and family. Gui left and went to work.

Without leaving a physical trace, every last bit of Gui's belongings were packed and dropped off at his penthouse. She had a set of keys, and had let herself in. To her disclosure, Shamha lived there and was lying in bed, at the time. Shamha, was shocked by Jan's appearance, and swiftly put on some appropriate clothes. Jan felt upset about freely entering the house, and sincerely apologised. However, the ladies amicably sat down for a heart-to-heart, over cups of tea. Shamha explained – it was a good intention that turned bad. They planned to have a baby, for Gui to share with Jan, so they could have a complete family. But they fell in love – and it changed everything. Shamha, felt guilty and hope Jan could be a part of the baby's life – should Jan and Gui, still wanted to have a family. Nevertheless, since Jan and Gui's relationship was over, she gave Shamha her blessings. They came to acknowledge that, they were only two sweet ladies, who got caught up in Gui's web, instead of normal couple's love nest.

Gui, was back in his own home with Shamha – but he didn't have the guts to tell her, about his one-night stand and sexually transmitted diseases. So Shamha felt totally responsible, for Gui and Jan's separation – and struggled to live with the damage done, to their relationship. A week later, she accessed Jan's mobile number, from Gui's phone and rang her.

Shamha pleaded for forgiveness, and encouraged Jan, to give Gui another chance. Jan assured her, there was nothing to worry about. She had done her, the biggest favour. Shamha was amazed, by Jan's calmness – and her easy-going attitude, was enough for Shamha to be consumed with guilt. However, Jan was happy, Gui was out of her life, and would like it to remain that way. Now, she had a lot of time to focus on other things – church, work and divorce. They had decided, there was no need to split their assets and finances – as they both had enough money.

Two years on, and single life was Jan's thing. Jan's splintering heartbreak, was worse than her first. Nonetheless, she recognised that, like everything else in life – relationships and marriages, come with their own mountains and valleys. However, Jan endeavoured to give God the glory, for her strength. In some ways, there was a great sense of relief. And despite all, she managed to stay afloat, in a positive way. A smile for her employees and friends always, without the sound of Gui's name.

Many questions waved through my mind,
But only this one I asked,
Of all the things that could be wrong,
Why, must my heart aches for so long?
In my dreams, the answer came,
Linger not in your past,
Though, must go and seek your path.
Only then you will see, what love has laden out for you,
And your days, may no longer be blue.

CHAPTER 9

A dying wish

Little did Jan knew, it wasn't quite over. One day, Shamha rang Jan and told her, she was terminally ill. She straight away, asked Jan if she could take her son, and be his mum. She trusted, Jan could love him, like he was her own. At the time, Jan was out with a few of her colleagues – at a housewarming party. She asked to be excused, and continued with the phone call from Shamha, in private. To her surprise, Shamha was diagnosed with motor neurone disease. Jan was astounded by the news. A tongue tied Jan, stuttered to apologise – but did, for as many times as she could. She simply didn't know what to say. But with immense bravery, Shamha continued to explain, her muscles were rapidly deteriorating, and so only had months left to live. What else to do, but to be empathetic and offer kind support? Precisely, what Jan did. Straight away, she went to see Shamha at their home. Gui met Jan at the door, a strange moment shared, as they were seeing each other again, for the first time since… Gui politely, invited her inside and offered a hot drink. Jan asked to see Jun-li, named after his Chinese grandfather. He was the spitting image of his dad. Jan gave a soft smile, as she gently stroked his cheeks, and his tiny hands. She quietly whispered, "He is beautiful."

Back in the living room, they sat down on the sofas – except for Shamha, who was sitting in her wheelchair. She, thanked Jan for coming over. And explained, she had extended family living nearby. Her parents, older and younger siblings, were living in another village, only a mile away. They were happy to help Gui take care of Jun-li, but she would like him to have a mother. Someone, who would love him infinitely, and do all the fun things a mum would do. Money wasn't an issue, and she doubted, it would ever be. There was only one request.

Jan stared Gui in his eyes, and quite confidently asked for his thoughts, regarding her involvement with Jun-li. Gui emphasized, he just wanted to fulfilled a dying wish. However, he knew it was a lot to ask. Gui added, they didn't need to be in a relationship – or share the same home, if Jan was saying yes. Also, they would be happy with doing a legal adoption. Jan could not believe, she heard the word adoption came of Gui's mouth. Time was of the essence, but Jan knew, she had to take some time to think carefully, if this was her burden to share and bare. She probed Shamha to tell more about her diagnosis, care and end of life's plans. She explained, motor neurone disease is an unusual condition, where aspects of the nervous system are damaged, without obvious reasons of how and why. As a result, muscles became weakened and consistently wasted. It has a major effect on the spinal cord and nerves cells, as these became ceased. Motor neurons, are responsible for motor skills, such as walking, talking and breathing. Also, eating, swallowing and holding things using our hands. The weakness, rapidly progress, and of such, the ability to feel and live normally, slowly disappears.

There is no cure, though medical practitioners ensured, a breathing mask and food tubes were in place, for when needed. So far, she was unable to walk, and swallow the usual amount of food. Despite it was noticeable, she slurred just a bit – however, the ability to speak was still much appreciated. Shamha was looking incredibly thin, she had lost a lot of weight, from ten to seven stones. She explained – it all started when Jun-li was only a few months old. Shamha discovered her hands, wasn't gripping Jun-li's hand. In that instant, she thought it was a strange thing to have happened. Shamha went to see her doctor – he presumed it might have been trapped nerves. Nevertheless, there was no hesitation, she was straight away referred to see a specialist. Her specialist, had the weirdest facial expression, as if she knew precisely... On that day, a scan was done on Shamha's hand – which had concluded MND.

Shamha had done further scans – included brain scans. By then, other parts of her body were getting weaker. By the time it got to her legs, Shamha had lost the ability to walk. Moving her head up and down, wasn't to be any more either. She expressed a strong sense of humiliation, distress and anger – as taking care of her beautiful short black hair, and shiny white teeth, were slowly becoming another person's job.

Shamha had given up her job. Thank God, Gui had decided to do one thing right. He stood by her. Gui had started working part-time, so he could spend more memorable time with them. They did a lot of travelling, and all the things listed on her bucket list. A few to mention, they travelled all the continents, even if not all the countries, helicopter rides, grand cruises, and met the queen. They took Jun-li to many places, and fitted in a great number of fun things. Although, when Jun-li is older, he perhaps won't remember much. However, there were plenty of photos and videos to show him. And as for Gui, surely, despite how daunting this was, he will remember the best of times with her. And not forgetting Jun-li – their greatest gift of all.

Gui had showed her immense love, kindness and support. Included paid for all the equipment she needed, private palliative care practitioners, psychotherapist, speech and language therapist and a buddy assistant. Her buddy assistant was a lady, who assisted with social care. Took her out for walks, had good conversations and lots of laughter. A nanny was hired, to help look after Jun-li. This was alongside, help from family and friends – who gave enormous support, the best they knew how. Shamha end of life plan was an open topic. She wanted it to happen peacefully, with Jun-li and Gui by her side. In the meantime, Shamha did the little things, she could still do for herself. A fancy straw box was packed, with her dress and makeup – as well as, her order of service. She had left a space, for Gui and her family, to add to the day in their own special way. Her final request, was for her body to be cremated, and kept until Jun-li was 16 years old. It was her desire, that he should choose a special place to scatter it, and create his own memory.

"I lift my hat and even my hair to you, Shamha. You're incredible! It is heart-wrenching, to listen to you planned your final days, but who am I to feel – what I'm feeling right now? When you're being so brave about it all," said Jan.

Not only did she have herself to think about, but her son. The one person, she would give her last breath for, but that breath was slowly leaving her... And it wasn't her choice! However, it was too much for Jan to take in – and she went home. Later that night about 11, Jan rang Gui. He answered, although remained quiet. Laid on the bathroom floor, flushed, weakened and distraught, Jan cried for over an hour – without speaking a word. Finally, when she could breathe and speak properly, thank you and good night, were all she said – before hung up the phone. In the tic of seconds, Jan realised, Gui didn't get a chance to talk about, how he was coping. And so, she rang him back. He expressed a great depth of sadness – his emotional aches were paramount. The situation was like no other, he had ever experienced. Splashed the cash on all he could give, was the very least. However, to be totally involved in Shamha's daily care, was a different matter – he explained. Experiencing the same emotional turmoil, Jan and Gui agreed to be there for each other.

Next day, Jan went and visited the family. She gave them the answer, they all anticipated. Jan didn't have the courage, to not grant a dying lady her last wish. They were elated – and decided, Jan could start getting used to Jun-li, by visiting whenever she wanted. Straight away, Shamha called her lawyer, and got the legal paperwork on a roll. From there on, the ladies spared some time and got to know each other, as much as they could. However, they had fun bonding, in spite of the unusual family setting. Shamha had a dry sense of humour, and great valour. Together, they went to the Maiden University hospital, where Shamha took part in a clinical trial. This was her way, of leaving hope behind. Great hope that, they will find a cure for this incredible debilitating condition.

It was final…

Time had passed, and all was done. She passed away peacefully in her sleep, with her favourite boys laid next to her. For the first time, Gui managed to cry. He held his son so close to his chest, and cry until there were no more tears. He looked at Jun-li, and saw pure preciousness in his eyes. And remembered, just how beautiful his mum was – inside and out. However, it was only a matter of days, before the funeral. On the day, many of Shamha's family and friends, were there to celebrate her life. They made it a day to remember – just like she had asked. A video with Shamha enjoying life her way, was played at length. Everyone also had a chance to listen to messages, she had left for them. It was a day of mixed emotions – especially, when the final letter came up on screen.

My Beloved Gui,

If you're reading this letter, then you know I'm gone. Life isn't as long as we would like it to be. So please cherish every precious moment, you're allowed to see. Don't spend too much time mourning, as it will not bring me back. Instead, pull yourself together and fill your days with happiness. You had always wanted kids, now you can tick one off your list. I have no regrets meeting you, and have had Jun-li. But I regretted the pain, I had caused Jan – and it goes without saying. I got to know Jan, and loved her too.

Please take good care of our boy. All the things I wanted to say to him, are things you could timely share with him, for both of us. The day will come, when he'll ask many questions – now, you must be there for him always. My heart aches just to write this letter, but hey... That's life. Take comfort in knowing, you've touched my life immensely. My most precious moments, were with you. I can never explain the feeling, I had for you and Jun-li. It's beyond spoken, only my heart truly knows how this feels. My heart is suffused with the greatest feeling, it could ever bear, love... My love for you both.

I'm grateful for your kindness. If my love could move mountains – then you know, your life would be plain sailing. I wish you, Jan and Jun-li happiness. My final words are for my son. I loved you with my whole being. All I wanted for you, is pure happiness. So please go through life knowing that, you were my best love. I adored you baby, and I surely missed that smile of yours. And the tons of kisses, I gave you – my days were filled with them. Still, I yearned for more. But your daddy, new mummy-Jan, and the rest of our family, will now fill your days with these.

Sham, love xx

After the funeral, Jan and Gui, took Jun-li on a holiday to America. A holiday fit for a prince, as all a little boy could enjoy, was given. They made up stories about his mum, for him – though how tough it was. Every time they looked at his beautiful face, Jan cried. They wondered, how this could be, a young boy was left without his mummy. Jan and Gui knew, they could never replace his mum. Though, they endeavoured to give him, the best life possible.

I love you, were the word she said,
With the brightest twinkles in her eyes,
And the cutest, wide smiles.
However, we might hope,
Long life isn't owed to us,
So be kind to one another,
And live life, without much fuss.
Though, how troubled some days may be,
It makes no sense, be angry and weary,
With those you no longer see.
Just enjoy your time alive,
With love ones, who are before your eyes,
And kindly let love be.

Jun-li lived with Gui, though he spent equal time with Jan. He was a happy boy, and was well loved by his family. Gui was taking time out from relationships, and hoped to discover himself somehow. Jun-li, was his most important priority, and he continued to work as normal. Gui was very busy with all else, and didn't take time out for grieving. One day, he had an incline that, it would be great for him and Jan to see a psychiatrist. Perhaps, they could go through the grieving process together. It was a good idea! They went to therapy, for approximately seven months. Jan had attended some additional sessions, on her own. This had helped them to also understand, each other motives and intentions, better than before. Jan told Gui, she was pleased to see him being the man, she once married – because there were days, he appeared to be the devil himself. Also, she had something else to be said, quite honestly.

"I went through some of your stuff, after our separation. And was totally astonished, by what I had found. I never spoke about them, because I was too scared. But blood thirsting…? What the hell is that?" Jan asked, with an expression of disgust. There was silence from Gui, as he took some deep breaths.

"I've read the published article, about your blood craving! Also that, you were a part of an investigation – for the murder of an old woman. I only saw bits of these articles – and so, I didn't get the whole story," Jan spoke, in a rather sharp tone.

It seemed his main heart-string was pulled, as he crossly replied…

"I don't kill for blood or anything of the sort. The newspapers spread propaganda. As you know, I do films... Horror films. I like blood in that respect. It inspires me to come up with new ideas. Besides, my workmates did that article as a joke on me, and it got out of control with the media."

"Okay...?" Jan said, using that sarcastic tone, to show her disbelief.

"Regarding the old woman, Vaisy Sohares, her grandson and a friend scenario... It was an accident. One that shouldn't have happened. I'm forever haunted by the outcome!" He said.

Jan was astonished, when she heard the names...

"Vaisy and Ethan's accident...! What did you have to do with that? Oh Noo... Noo... It wasn't you. Please say it wasn't." Jan exclaimed.

"Oh... You heard about that? Well... it was on the news. Please, let me explain all," Gui responded eagerly.

"I had a jug of blood, on the front passenger seat of the car. I thought the lid was on tightly, but it wasn't. And so it spilled. I took my eyes off the road for a second to stop it from spilling... Aaaw... That awful smell! When suddenly my car hit their car. I was in a state of shock, so I did the wrong thing, swerved and kept driving. The blood, it was lamb's blood. I got it from a butcher, but something wasn't right about it. The smell was just awful."

"I was the friend in that car!!! My life hasn't been the same since... I had nightmares for many months – even flashbacks, just remembering it all! I have to live with this horrific image every day, just knowing I was driving the car. It's almost as if, I was responsible for all that had happened. Could you imagine, how I'm feeling? They were my family once! What have you done? What have you done?" She spoke out furiously.

"You are a very stupid man...! You silly old bat...! Perhaps, there aren't any words to describe your incredible heartlessness! A life has been lost, and another changed significantly – because of your recklessness!" Jan shouted.

Gui was just as astonished, as Jan. He suddenly opened his eyes wide, stared at Jan, with the most confused and frustrated looks, in his eyes. He despairingly stood up and placed his hands on his head, before unexpectedly broke down in tears, at Jan's feet – momentarily lost for words. Gui consistently cried out, I'm sorry!!! But it wasn't enough for Jan. She secretly dialed 999, whilst the phone was in her trousers' pocket. Then got him to tell her about the accident again, as it was recorded by the police.

"Oh My Gosh Gui! I'm terrified of you! Never knew you! ... Don't think I want to know you anymore! So sorry, I didn't know all these things, before our marriage!" Jan cried out angrily.

"There is no need to live in fear. I never intended to hurt you Jan. Let's get one thing straight, I'm not a vampire or a bloodsucker or anything of the sort. Physically, I do nothing with blood. Another thing Honey, I would never do anything to hurt you again, you are my one true love. I deeply regretted it... And I will regret it for the rest of my life. I would like you, to please believe me! Please... Accidents happen! Sorry!" Gui shouted out.

Jan spoke at Gui and said – she will one day forgive him, for Jun-li's sake. But right now, they deserve a quiet life. Gui, nodded his head and agreed.

"Thank you so much, Jan. Not just for your forgiveness, but for everything. You are amazing! I love you and Jun-li."

Jan turned herself away from him, when suddenly they heard a hearty-knocking at the door – it was the police. Gui looked at Jan, with shocking disbelief. Jan told him, she will take good care of Jun-li, but he should not to expect visits.

Days after Gui's breaking news, there was a public update on Ethan's progress. He was fully recovered, became a Christian, and got married to his pregnant wife. They were living in Jamaica, near his parents. Ethan was also the proud owner, of his new fashion designing school. Being the lovely person Ethan was, he had given his parents sufficient money and a nice home. All-in-all, they had life at its best.

Jan was relieved to hear, things had turned out so well for Ethan, in the end. And with all the additional information, Ethan gave in his news interview, Jan felt he was sending her a message. And if so, it worked. Since then, Jan had peace of mind, knowing he was happy and well.

Time allow us to start so many things,
That we may never get the chance to complete,
So, whether it's to lend a hand,
Or sing praises to our King,
Let's use it wisely,
And be content, with the best of what it brings.

CHAPTER 10

Utmost Love

Months later, Jan anticipated starting a new chapter. However, she contemplated, how to be super careful with her heart. Recent months, Jan had definitely showed interest in John, the main minister of the church, she was attending. And of course, there were those niggling questions in her mind. *Why do I even want to love again? Haven't I, been through enough?* But if Jan had acknowledged anything, it would be the idea that life goes on. Furthermore, all men aren't made up of the same genes. Perhaps, some people were born to be deceitful, and not many are prone to understand, acknowledge and accept what love really is.

Very few moments past, when Jan hadn't felt a great need for intimacy. Though she embraced patience, courage and strength – it didn't make her need any less. To be loved again meant everything to Jan.

How battered I may be, by others evilness,
Still, I will find a way to rise again,
Shine even, and live life to its fullest.
My heart burns with aches,
And a sense of ancient longing,
My desire to be loved once more, surely isn't fake.
My mind, my body – my heart and my soul,

All in tune, for an answer from above,
As I wait, to meet him,
Hoping he knows, just how to love.

John had the utmost admiration, for Jan – and was totally smitten. Everyone could see, except Jan. Jan knew, she had felt a connection, but didn't know, if John had felt it too. Despite, John had invested much time and effort, in speaking to her. Even, when there wasn't anything significant to be talked about. He frequently gazed at her, most pleasantly – and trusted, Jan would see the signs and respond to them. However, because John was seemingly confident, everyone thought, he would have already told Jan about his feelings. Instead, he had played it safe, and fore-fronted shyness.

Though, I stood in front of thousands,
And preached the words,
My heart is in constant flutter,
When your face stood out, in the midst of the crowd.
I may close my eyes when praying,
But I sure do imagine your beautiful face, getting close to mine,
So Darling, please give me your utmost love,
And let our hearts be entwined.

One Saturday afternoon, Jan went and did her weekly shopping, at Dingoss supermarket. She had picked up all her usual things, and was just wandering around the pastry aisle. A can of chicken soup fell out of her shopping basket. She stooped quite gracefully, to pick the can up. But a nice long and slender arm, stretched forth and got it for her. She straightened up in slow motion, and looked to her right – it was John from the church. They smiled and said hello. John, gazed into Jan's eyes, while he put the canned soup into her basket. Jan flicked her hair, before she told him thanks, for such kind gesture.

"Do you come here often?" John said, quite pleasantly.

"Eerm yes, this is where I come every week... To do my weekly..." Jan replied.

"... And what about you?" Jan asked.

"Yes, most times. The odd weekends or so, I go over to Southway..."

"Oh, right! It's quite a shop, Southway... Mainly for the upper class," Jan said endearingly. They both laughed.

"I go for the long drive... Quite a scenic route," said John – sounded modest.

"OK..." Jan nodded her head and replied. As she flicked her hair.

"Oh, eerm, I best get going now. It was lovely seeing you Jan," said John.

"Aan... And you," Jan responded with a smile.

John elegantly walked towards the cash register, and joined the queue. Jan gazed at him – and paid close attention, to his buttocks. However, John somehow didn't seem quite at ease. He looked back at Jan, and took a deep breath. He suddenly walked towards her, and asked...

"Might we, be able to see each other again?"

Jan, was startled by that thought. Though she swiftly responded, and told him yes.

"Bye again," John said, rather charmingly. And this time, he made his way passed the cash register. Jan laughed softly, and told him...

"I think, the cash register is to your right."

He smiled, nodded at her, and went to pay for his groceries. Jan had turned her face to the pastry counter, whilst pretended she was just about to order. She then waited a moment, for John to leave the supermarket completely, before paying for her groceries and went home.

> Shyness may cause delayed reaction, but it certainly doesn't stand in the way of love.

A while after being back home, Jan went out to her back garden for a moment of solitude. She heard a slight sound, in Sandy's back garden and wondered... A moment of inquisitiveness, she went and took a peek over the fence, and saw a gentleman – it was Ernie. He was the spitting image of John. Jan was astounded – as she had some flashing thoughts.

"What's John doing by Sandy, she whispered to herself? I didn't know they had met."

She stood with her back against the wooden fence in awe. Jan slowly reached for her mobile phone and texted Sandy. "Is that John, by you Sandy?"

"It's not John. It's my friend Ernie, who had been away for several years, before you and I met," Sandy texted back.

"Oh, right... I thought that, I was having a deja vu kind of a day. His voice is so like John's, even his looks... Oh My Gosh, never have I seen this... Today is definitely an interesting day," Jan text back.

"Would you like to meet him? We could come over and join you in the garden. Only if you want to," Sandy talked with Jan, from the other side of the fence.

"Of course, please come over."

As she anticipated meeting Ernie. Sandy approached the garden gate, and both of them went over to Jan.

"Jan, this is Ernie... My long lost friend. The prodigal son returned," Sandy sounded delightful.

"Hello, so nice to meet you. Please sit down and make yourselves comfortable. Can I interest you in something to drink?" Jan politely asked, while slightly admiring Ernie.

"Yes, please. Water would be good," Ernie, responded courteously.

"Great, I will get us some drinks and nibbles," Jan politely suggested.

While Jan was getting the food together, she was chatting away openly to Sandy.

"So Sandy, how is it you had never mentioned Ernie before?" Jan asked.

"It's interesting, she likes to keep her friends on separate pages... She never mentioned you either Jan. Thank graciousness for today," Ernie said, politely.

"Oh, don't give me a hard time guys, I just never get the chance to... But here, I have done it now... Haven't I?" Sandy said, as they all burst into laughter.

"I supposed so, Sandy. How convenient?" Jan, pleasantly responded.

Jan couldn't stop herself from thinking, how incredible similar John and Ernie were. However, she left that thought to rest – and offered drinks and snacks from a selection, while they talked about friendship. Sandy and Ernie first met, one winter afternoon, when Ernie was walking home soaking wet. Sandy, had a spare jumper in her school bag, and hesitated not to lend it to him. They were living in the same village, but not near each other. So from that day, Sandy and Ernie became best friends.

Every Saturday afternoon, Sandy and Ernie would have a picnic, or played netball on the park court. But a beautiful teenage friendship was worn out, just after six months. Ernie had to go away, and lived with his dad and stepmother in Canada. For the first few months, they wrote to each other. One month it was Sandy's turn to receive her letter, and it didn't come. From thereafter, there were no more letters. Now, Ernie was back – he went to Sandy's childhood home. And the neighbours, who were still good friends with Sandy, gave Ernie her address. Sandy, was amazed to see Ernie. She stood in the front garden, scooping up small piles of dried leaves – fallen off the blossom trees. Suddenly, her eyes glanced at the gate, and saw Ernie closely approaching…

"Hello beautiful!" Ernie said.

There was a familiar face, Sandy thought – although she wasn't quite sure, if it was Ernie.

"Of course, it's the first person who came into her thoughts. Have you forgotten me?" Said Ernie.

She softly exclaimed, "Erns! Ernie oh my! I can't believe we met again. You're back?"

Ernie burst into laughter, as they hurried towards each other and hugged. Just before Jan disrupted them… Ernie conversed with Sandy, he was taking time out to see his family. He hadn't seen them since his wife Amy left, four years ago – when they had last visited… Amy walked out on Ernie, because he couldn't fulfill her sexual desires. One day, she had an outburst and told him, they were over. She had spent too many years, waited for him to grow up in the private department. However, the longer they stayed together, it was becoming more apparent he was unable to be practical. Nonetheless, Ernie thought things were alright, since she was spending his money on sex toys that could replace him. There was no turning back for Amy, she had taken her two kids (10 year-old son, Zane and 8 year-old daughter, Shez) and left. Ernie and Amy, didn't share biological kids – Amy didn't want to have anymore – so Ernie happily accepted her wish, over his desire to have kids.

So it was interesting when both Jan and Ernie, took interests into each other lives. Ernie was happy to share that, he hoped to love again. Sandy spotted something, she looked at them simultaneously and smiled. It was as if, there was an instant attraction. There was something, electric, magnetic even! However, she didn't add fuel to the fire – and just enjoyed a great afternoon.

Monday morning – Jan and Sandy were just about leaving, to go to work. They greeted each other at the fence, bordered their homes. Sandy told Jan, Ernie would be coming by again soon, and would like to take her out on a date – if she will. Jan replied yes, she would like to meet up with Ernie – and it was alright for Sandy to give Ernie her mobile number. During her lunch break, Jan went to a nearby cafe. Once Jan ordered her

Panini, fresh green salad, and orange juice – she took her diary, turned to a clean page, and wrote FRESH START. However, later that evening, Jan and Sandy conversed over the telephone…

"Jan, I am still at work – and won't be at the practice till late today. So I'll be home before long – maybe we could talk about some dating stuff, later," said Sandy.

"That sound like a plan, Sand… Because I'm thinking of fixing a date with John, soon," Jan voiced.

"Go for it, Jan. But what about Ernie?"

Despite, Sandy wasn't keen on her friends becoming partners, this one was slightly out of her control.

"I… I don't know for sure – maybe we could meet too, and see how it goes," Jan replied.

Sunday morning – church as usual. During the meet and greet session, John had greeted Jan with a hug – and then placed a note in her hand. He looked at her charmingly and smiled, before he went on to greet others. Jan slowly excused herself from the main room, and went to the lavatory. She read the note. It stated…

> *Hello Jan, we only know each other through church. Yet, I found myself thinking about you so much, I'm now forced by my emotions, to let you know… I'm age 38 and single as you're aware. Every day that passed me by, I hoped that God would reveal, the queen that he had prepared for me. Would you be so kind enough to go out on a date with me? Even if it's just one date – one time, should give us an idea, if we're a match for each other. Love, John.*

Jan felt tentative, now that John came forth and made his feelings known. Jan knew there was an important choice to be made. However, she went back inside the main hall, and anxiously enjoyed the service. Afterwards, Jan went to see John. They both looked somewhat nervous – although, put forth their best smiles. Jan had written her mobile and house numbers on a notepad sheet, and gave it to him. Later that evening, John rang Jan. First, they talked about the church, then eventually got on to the topic, of how they were feeling. John described his feelings, as tingles inside his stomach. Also, they were deeper, than he had ever felt before. Jan was besieged – she had no idea, he felt so strongly about her, up until then.

Jan considered him a nice man, who could be worthy of her love and loyalty. John was asked, to explicate his feelings towards her present family life – regarding her son, in particular. He believed, together they could make a nice family – and he would be happy with Jun-li, as his stepson. John went on to talk about his half-brother, who only had step-children – but was back from Canada visiting. Something tingled Jan's ears – this was a familiar story.

"Is your brother called Ernie?" Jan curiously asked.

Felt strangely surprised by the confirmation, Jan asked for them to pause, for a few seconds – as she took deep breaths, and gathered her thoughts.

"Sure, is it something I've said?" John anxiously asked.

"No. You are ok... Erm, do you know my friend Sandy?"

"I only know one Sandy – she's Erns best friend. They were recently re-united, and I've never seen him so lit-up," said John.

Jan giggle, politely...

John asked, what was funny. She replied, by telling him a little more about herself and Sandy. As well as, she had met her brother and felt a slight connection with him.

John gave a surprised laugh – as he talked about their brotherly closeness, despite they were different fathers. Nonetheless, Jan and John enjoyed a few moments of laughter – but continued to talk some more. John was very keen on setting a date with Jan. Therefore, they agreed to meet at his home, 1pm the following Saturday. They ended their conversation, on a high note.

Jan had a lot of time to digest, such a weekend. However, she wasted no time – and rang Ernie. Jan asked him to meet with her sooner. Monday was a good day, as Jan was off work. Ernie had suggested, he will stop by about 10am.

Monday morning, Ernie was right on time – as soon as the door buzzer went, Jan was straight to the door.

"Hello Ernie, nice to see you again," Jan politely greeted him.

They hugged delicately and kissed on the cheeks. She offered a drink, and he accepted coffee – and requested it to be strong. Soon after, they went to the living room, where they sat comfortably and conversed. Jan communicated to Ernie, how she felt the day they met. But the question got be asked...

"Have you spoken to John?" Jan asked.

"Yes, we've spoken… And I also have to admit, I loved you, the moment we were introduced."

Jan felt awkward, as she had to tell him, his brother was chosen. Ernie was deeply disappointed, though he assured Jan, he was OK – and wished them true happiness. Nevertheless, Jan suggested they relax and get to know each other. Between them, there was so much to talk about, Ernie stayed for lunch. However, Ernie was still wondering, why Sandy didn't tell Jan, he was John's brother. Jan explained, Sandy heard her talking about John from church, but she didn't know it was Ernie's John. She hadn't yet introduced Sandy, to whom she was always talking about.

Overall, Jan felt pleased with her choice. Somehow, there was a little voice in her mind giving assurance, John was the man for her. Even though, John had never had a proper relationship, since he became a Christian in his late teens. He was waiting on God, to show him his queen.

It was John and Jan date weekend. Jan wore an ankle length, body-fitted, slim straps, red and black dress, and a pair of black killer heels shoes, with matching purse. Arrived at the house, Jan greeted John, and gave him a bottle of chateau Pipeau Saint Emilion wine. Looked very smart, John wore a slim-fitted, blue and white plod shirt, black trousers, and very trendy black shoes. Not only was Jan greeted by John, but also his dogs Flash and Rex. They took a shine to Jan, and offered her paw-shakes.

"Well, if you passed the test with my dogs, then surely your place is already secured in our family," John spoke jokily.

John showed Jan around his lovely home, just before he led the way to his office – rearranged to accommodate its momentary purpose. Jan didn't know what to expect, but when the door was opened, she stood in awe. It was short of nothing for a romantic date. The window blinds were half tilted, the room was lit up with scented candles, beautifully arranged – alongside the most attractive floral bouquet in a vase. A date without a special gift for the lady, may not be possible – as John presented to Jan, a box of handmade champagne truffles, with a red bow on top.

The ambiance was set with soft instrumental music, played to the tune of Regina Bell and Pebo Bryson. Jan looked a little nervous, as she was seated at the table. They got started with water and pineapple juice. But it wasn't long, before they tucked into a three-course lunch meal. Starter, mouth-watering open-cup stuffed mushrooms, with cheese and bacon. The main meal was celeriac mash, roasted sea bass, on a bed of steamed green vegetables and cream sauce. And dessert was tantalising, white chocolate-raspberry tart. John aimed to impress, and had prepared the entire three courses. And impressed Jan was – with the immense effort and time, John had put into their first date.

Their conversation started off light and entertaining – John talked about some of his funniest childhood moments, silly haircuts and his pathetic shyness. Jan shared her most treasured memories – holidays with Jim. Finally, the main topic of the day surfaced – their aim for a new relationship.

"Look at us today, on a date… It feels surreal. I remember when I first realised that, I like you very much. It was about seven months ago. But I was nervous about telling you. My parents, two sisters, two brothers, three nieces and four nephews, all knew I can't stop thinking about you," said John.

Jan smiled and shared, "It was about four months ago, I realised that I find you very attractive, inside and out."

After lunch, John had another surprise for Jan. Hence, he led the way to a mild river, which was located at the end of his estate. It was about a mile away – secluded, tranquil and beautiful. Awaited them in the warm sun, was a lovely two-seater roof-hammock – right at the bank of the river, under a big oak tree. There was a straw basket, packed with cooked olives, fresh strawberries, water and a single red rose. They ate, swung and relaxed for another hour – with only the marvellous sounds of cooing birds and running streams. It was the perfect date. However, after about an hour, they timely walked back to John's home. In conversation, they agreed to do it again really soon. At the gate, John gently kissed Jan on her cheeks, and said goodbye.

Back at home, Jan relaxed in her living room, and watched dirty dancing. She texted Sandy and gave an updated.

"Will you give John a chance, then?" Sandy replied.

"John is worthy of a chance – and I am happy to be falling in love again," said Jan.

Just before Jan's bedtime, her mobile phone beeped – John had texted (*I was just checking, you got home safely*).

Jan responded, by phoning John. They conversed at length – mostly, they talked about their day, and then finally agreed to another date. Jan wished John a pleasant night, and hoped they won't be awkward at church the next day.

Sunday morning, Jan went to church as usual. There were definitely a lot of eye-catching moments, between Jan and John. During meet and greet session, they hugged as usual – while Jan slipped a note into his jacket pocket. He was invited to her place for dinner. After church, she went straight home, prepared dinner and freshened up. John hadn't appeared on time – Jan was quite uneasy and became doubtful. She wondered if this was just another dark hole, awaited her. Soon, the buzzer went – John was finally there. Jan hurried to the door and greeted him, with a kiss on the cheeks. She invited him inside, and gave a tour. John asked many questions, mainly about the outstanding achievement awards, in the library.

"Let's answer these questions, while we eat our starter – mains are in the oven, and dessert will be whenever you are ready," Jan spoke anxiously.

To start, they licked their fingers, eating pan-cooked prawns in lemon sauce. Followed by crusty roasted potatoes, roasted lamb, gravy and green beans. Then finally, they indulged in delicious Eton mess – of which, John delightfully had double portions. There were lots of compliments at the table – while they toasted their new beginning, with champagne. After dinner, they relaxed and filled the evening with laughter – shared funny jokes, and embarrassing moments. Jan, shared her most shameful moment.

"When I was about 18, I went on a camping trip. It was held on a college campus, for a week. But this particular night, I dreamt, I couldn't find my favourite pair of knickers. So, when I woke up in the morning, I searched – and realised that I couldn't find them, indeed. I alerted the entire dormitory, then only to eventually found them, just where I had left them. I had washed and hung them on a knickers hanger, outside to dry – but had forgotten to bring them inside, before I went to bed. Everyone, had seen that I had found them. So I couldn't make an excuse – after all the drama, I had created. Totally embarrassed, I was!"

Jan didn't want to spend the entire afternoon, at her place. Therefore, she offered for them to see, *One in a Million* – a romantic movie, at the cinema. It was about a couple, who found perfection in each other flaws. Throughout the two-hour film, they shared a mega bucket of popcorn and a large soda – topped up with frequent soft gazes and gentle cuddles. They seemed at ease, like a pair of old socks – when the evening was over, they went back to their separate homes.

On their third date, Jan had booked a twin room – which apparently meant separate beds, at one of London's most prestigious hotels. The weekend started off with breakfast, followed by spa treatments. During this time John seemed vacant, uncertain of what to do next. But Jan, was one step ahead, and pulled out two surprise tickets for a football game (Lifters vs Nothics), John really wanted to attend, but chose their date instead. John felt very grateful, Jan was so thoughtful. At the end of the day, they relaxed in the hotel lounge with some drinks – before headed off to bed.

It was now official, they were an item. Only this time, John preferred marriage before sex. But a wedding, might not be the next thing on Jan's mind, just yet. However, it was quite fundamental for the church members, to know of their relationship. Hence, John made it known to all... Other people to be told, were Gui and Jun-li. Gui sometimes called from the prison, he was serving 25 years. Jan had a chance to let him know, she was moving on with John. And assured him, Jun-li was still her main priority. Gui expressed, kind and supportive thoughts towards Jan. He also appreciated that, she was a great mum to Jun-li, and they wouldn't exchange her for the world. Jan was chuffed to hear those words, and it motivated her to continue. Jan reflected on her life so far – amazed by the constant changes – she whispered to herself, "time to move on to happy land."

Two months later, Jan had arranged for Jim and John to meet, at her home. Jim went over and spent a week, with the aim of getting to know John. Jim had no reason to stand in Jan's way – hence, gave them his blessings. He was satisfied with John, as a minister and youth counsellor.

Jan and John dated for one and a half years, and were engaged for 11 months. After such long courtship, wedding plans were in full swing. They decided on pink and cream, theme colours. All hands were on deck, as John's family showed their love and support – likewise Jim. This time around, John and Jan were in control of their wedding arrangements. They also made time, and squeezed in a full-body beauty session, just before the day. Meanwhile, members of their church, decorated the wedding hall to suit. The floral arrangement was attractive – beautiful and lavish, were the words to describe... The bridal party included – Sandy (maid of honour), John sisters (bridesmaids) and nieces (junior bride's maids and mini bride). John's brothers Ernie, Brent and his best friend Andrew (groom's men) and Jun-li (page boy). And of course, it wouldn't be quite special, without their parents – as they witnessed their eldest son got married. And Jim, father of the bride twice.

The regional director of the church, was their master of ceremony. He kept it short and lovely. However, all eyes were on the couples' rings and outfits. Jan's wedding band was stunning –attractive white gold, 21 carat sapphire, pink diamond ring. And most certainly, only the best wedding gown for Jan. Her cream fitted, and very eye-catching gown, glittered with diamonds and pearls, was a cut above the rest – worthy of its £250,

000. John was happy with his £15,500, five-piece cream suite (with pink cravat), and matching cream shoes. John's wedding band was stunning too – similar to Jan's... A big summer reception, at a Dela Grande Palace in the country sides, had completed their evening. The atmosphere was just as they desired – perfect! Jan handed Sandy her pink and cream posy bouquet, instead of traditionally throwing it for a random catch. After all, the very tall, handsome and muscly John, was left to enjoy his gorgeous wife. The next day, Mr and Mrs Xinguti went to Jamaica for three weeks, and had a wonderful honeymoon.

The newlywed moved in together, the night after their wedding. They had sold their individual homes, and bought a 10 bedroom mansion in Surrey. Everything was brand new, and fitted into place perfectly. Six weeks later, Jan woke up one morning, and was feeling very sick – yet, she went to work and fainted upon arrival. Jan was transported to the hospital, where she discovered, she was pregnant with quadruplets. The news spread fast – Gui was amongst, the first set of people to be told. Totally astonished by the news, Gui struggled to say congratulations. However, he thought it was only fair, to give Jan full access to his finances, to support Jun-li'.

The happy parents to be, celebrated for weeks – just utterly overwhelmed, by it all. They got themselves into protective mode – Jan had given up working full-time, though kept her business blooming. John was the perfect husband, they had a calmer, less erotic sex life – although a happy and fulfilled one. However, other aspects of their lives, were about to change significantly, as Jan and John, prepared mentally and emotionally to become parents, to five children. Together, they acknowledged, there will be huge responsibilities – and perhaps, pressure and high expectations from various others. Nevertheless, they were determined to do their best – with a lot of support from their families.

Two and half months later, baby Janis, Jiani, Jona and James arrived. Mother and babies were well. And days, even months followed, they were overwhelmed with love and support – from everyone. Nonetheless, they continued to enjoy a very opulent lifestyle, and had fulfilment at its best. Jim had sold his house one final time, and bought a six bedroom bungalow, with plenty of space for his grand kids. Jun-li was the proud big brother, who had given his siblings a lot of love. And if everyone didn't know, he wasn't Jan's biological child, then no one would have guessed. Jan and John, adored him. John was a great dad, to all five children – despite his own personal flaws.

Sixteen years later, Jan, John and their large family, were still living happily together. They had encountered, many mountainous hills and deep valleys. But joy lived in the midst of their lives, as they strengthened each other – and worked as a team, to overcome their troubles. Their hearts, strength and minds became one, and formed a relationship that was cemented in God – and reflected Utmost love, entirely.

I would do anything for your happiness,
Even, if your obstacles seem impossible,
I will be your Mr incredible.
My arms and ears, I will avail,
So you know, my warmth is always there.

You are my one true love,
And to say I love you, is never enough,
To justify the way I feel about you.
My heart is overwhelmed with something deeper,
Than words can express.
But I promise to do my best, in showing you what I mean,
Every time, I let you feel my delicate touch.
I hope you know, in all big and small gestures,
I have filled them up with much more love,
Than your heart can feel, and your eyes can see.
My darling, my strongest love is for you always,
And it remains this way, every single day.

CHAPTER 11

Poetry speaks volume

I look to Thee

Lift me up, oh Lord,
For my face, is towards the ground,
Let my eyes, see the light,
And my heart and soul sing your praises, in one accord.
Give me strength, to speak thy words,
As they are my only swords,
Let me remember these days, when your mercies,
Unto me, you gave,
And my life you've saved.
Oh God, lift me up on high,
As I look to you, in the bright blue skies.

Forgiveness

Learn to forgive each other,
Not just your sister or your brother,
But everyone, as all belong to our father.
Your heart is unfathomable,
Capable of holding all the things that, make you comfortable.
Hesitate not, to make room for love,
Or your heart will be plagued with savagery,
It's much better with great things that, won't let you have to worry.
Fill it with contentment and joyfulness,
Even some warmth,
And a little kindness.

A prayer a day

The simple things, she had always said,
Pray to God, before you go to bed,
He has provided a comfortable place, to rest your weary head.
As you walk the road of life,
Don't ever forget faith, hope and peace,
These are things, your heart should surely keep.
Live in love and harmony,
And stress not yourself, if there isn't sufficient money,
As it will only last for a while,
And happiness is for a lifetime.

Life

Oh Lord, I pray,
For guidance and strength each day,
Lest, I rely on my own will and astray.
Teach me father, to be humble and kind,
Because it's your will and not mine.
Oh God, please let me continuously seek thy face,
It's the only place, I find saving grace.
I prayed for you to dwell more in me,
Dear Lord, as I pray these simple words to Thee.

Let's pray

Let me learn to listen to your still voice,
This I know, will take me through the darkest night,
Let me hear your voice, oh Lord…
As words spoken, will be my light…

My heart rejoices

I will sing your praises, all day long,
I will sing the sweetest words, from my favourite songs.
I want the world to know, how great you are,
My God, you are my Supreme,
My ever shining guiding star.
So I will shout it out aloud,
Until your praises is heard, even through the clouds.

CHAPTER 12

A Letter to my husband and our three sons

Dearest Robin, Joshua, Jaden and Javier,

Robin, I love you so much more, than you will ever be able to comprehend. Your great wits and fabulous sense of humour, filled my days with laughter. You are sensitive, caring, loyal and kind. And I cherish the best of you. We've been through so much together. And I'm grateful to God for strengthening us. I rained all my love, hugs and kisses in this letter for you.

Life certainly is filled with surprises, both good and bad. Boys, you will see this for yourself as you grow. It's also filled with wonderful blessings, and most certainly my darlings, you are without a shadow of a doubt, my greatest blessings. I Thank God for every un-promised day, we live to see. These days were and are my best days, my greatest moments. The days that are filled with life, love and laughter because of you. I never want to ever miss a moment in your lives, good or bad. Without your presence, my life is empty and meaningless.

My love for you is the most precious thing, my heart carries around constantly. Just like the blood that it pumps to keep me going. From the moment of conception, my love for you started unfolding, and still has so much more to go – as it is without end. It is ever so deep, and it's forever getting deeper and deeper. Through your existence, I have learned a different, more meaningful and profound love.

A love that is shared, amongst you in abundance. A love that allows me, to always make sure you are never unhappy. You are never in need… A love which propels me, to go the last mile of the way – and give my last breath for you, without thinking twice. It's a love like no other, it's beyond natural imagination. It's the love that comes out, when I smile at you… When I giggle at the silly things, which make you giggle. When I kiss you… When I worry about you… When I watch you sleeping… When I see you, met your milestones. When you are excited about something, anything or even nothing special… A love that makes me feel blue, when you are away for a moment. A love that makes me care endlessly. It's the kind of love that's most persistent – and assures me that, I would never give up on you. It's my love for you – that unceasingly flows, like a rushing river that never runs dry. My darlings, it's simply my best love for you – pure, free and uncomplicated infinite love.

I hope and wish for you all, to continue being happy. Life will teach you so many different lessons, and learning from them will be great. Take life as one gigantic opportunity, and embrace it the best you can. Knowing you're all very well loved, unconditionally. The things that make me happy, are seeing your smiles, giving you lots of love, precious care, tight hugs and sweet kisses (and believe me, I give a lot). Most of all, though I have made mistakes, my best is all I give to you each and every day. No matter, how big or small is the gesture. I give the best of myself, for your happiness. You are my Utmost love, the ones God has chosen for me. I am forever grateful to God, for all – but especially this wonderful privilege, He has given me. Please, love God first, as he first loves you. Give Him your best, as He gave his best for you.

Infinite love, hugs and kisses…

Wife and mum,
Tanya Frew.

I love you with all my being,
My heart isn't capable of giving any more,
As all it's possessed with, is what you have seen.
I am, who I am,
I'm not a perfect human being,
But I am determined to shine bright,
And be your sunbeam.
Everything I have got, belongs to you,
I could be stripped bare, and I would survive,
Purely because, for you – I can do…
I could be financially poor,
Eat and live like a pauper,
In exchange for my entrance, through your heart's door.
Baby, you are my sole desire,
The only one with the tools, to light my fire.
And I will stop at nothing, Dear,
Until the whole world knows, just how much I care.
I love you, is all I wanted to say,
And I will keep on saying it, every single day.

Lightning Source UK Ltd.
Milton Keynes UK
UKHW01f0531180518
322820UK00001B/22/P